Before he'd thou[...] through, Danil [...] tested his fingers against the soft skin of her cheek, her jaw, angling her head to soften her lips against his. To run his tongue across the seam of her mouth.

To taste.

Because she tasted like the sea. Crisp and promising. Deep and dark underneath the pretty, sparkling surface. It was meant to be a bit of a lark. To see exactly what Elsebet might offer and how he could use this surprising turn of events to complete his mission.

But the water was closing in over his head. Her kiss was potent, surprising, not what he'd prepared himself for. Her hands clutched his shirt, pressing herself closer. And his arms came around her waist, holding her securely. His fingers spread wide, spanning her waist. So slim, so delicate.

He was a tool. Heartless and soulless. More machine than man who needed no one and nothing. A kiss was a kiss, and nothing more.

But this was...not that. She was...innocent.

Meant for his *brother*.

Lorraine Hall is a part-time hermit and full-time writer. She was born with an old soul and her head in the clouds, which, it turns out, is the perfect combination to spend her days creating thunderous alpha heroes and the fierce, determined heroines who win their hearts. She lives in a potentially haunted house with her soulmate and rambunctious band of hermits-in-training. When she's not writing romance, she's reading it.

Books by Lorraine Hall

Harlequin Presents

The Prince's Royal Wedding Demand
A Son Hidden from the Sicilian

Secrets of the Kalyva Crown

Hired for His Royal Revenge
Pregnant at the Palace Altar

Visit the Author Profile page
at Harlequin.com.

Lorraine Hall

THE FORBIDDEN PRINCESS HE CRAVES

Recycling programs for this product may not exist in your area.

ISBN-13: 978-1-335-59301-6

The Forbidden Princess He Craves

Copyright © 2023 by Lorraine Hall

All rights reserved. No part of this book may be used or reproduced in any manner whatsoever without written permission except in the case of brief quotations embodied in critical articles and reviews.

This is a work of fiction. Names, characters, places and incidents are either the product of the author's imagination or are used fictitiously. Any resemblance to actual persons, living or dead, businesses, companies, events or locales is entirely coincidental.

For questions and comments about the quality of this book, please contact us at CustomerService@Harlequin.com.

Harlequin Enterprises ULC
22 Adelaide St. West, 41st Floor
Toronto, Ontario M5H 4E3, Canada
www.Harlequin.com

Printed in U.S.A.

THE FORBIDDEN
PRINCESS HE CRAVES

For Soraya. Thank you for your boundless enthusiasm.

CHAPTER ONE

PRINCESS ELSEBET THORE knew she was a princess, and as such her role in life was very simple. She was nothing more than a pawn to be used by her father, King of Mathav, to keep their tiny nation from being absorbed by the larger ones that surrounded it.

As such, Elsebet had been secluded on her father's private, secret island in the North Sea since she'd become *of* age. To protect her, he insisted.

Elsebet hadn't always been cognizant of *what* she was being protected from, considering her father had kept her under lock and key back at home, but at least on the island she had some sense of freedom. The staff was small, though devoted and more like family than staff. Because the island was so isolated, so unknown and so inaccessible because of its craggy peaks and inhospitable shoreline, she had some measures of liberty she'd never enjoyed back in Mathav.

She could walk the beaches alone, as she did this windy, stormy morning. She could nap in the library unchaperoned. She helped with chores, felt *useful* here, and sometimes, she could even make her own meals if she so wished. These were all things that never would have happened back at her father's castle in Mathav. She would have *always* had a chaperone, and never been allowed to do anything that might be viewed as beneath a princess.

It had taken her a while to appreciate this, but now she did. Unfortunately, regardless of what freedom she'd found here, she was twenty-two years old now and her entire adolescence had been spent on this island. Her only company the staff of three and her father when he visited.

She was lonely. She was bored. As she took her usual morning walk along the little alcove of sandy beach, searching for the seashells she had taken to making art murals out of just to have something to do, she looked out at the sea and wished for something other than what she had.

She had tried to express her restlessness to her father as a child. She knew he cared for her. He had, in fact, doted on her for most of her childhood. But the older she'd gotten, the more she'd looked like her late mother, the more she'd *expressed* her frustration, and the less she'd seen him. The more she'd demanded or cried or begged, the more certain and determined he'd become to keep her on this tiny island to await the political marriage that would help Mathav.

These days, she didn't even try to express her negative feelings, and he seemed content to believe that once he had chosen a husband for her, she would be too busy starting a family to want anything more.

Elsebet wished she could believe that. But marriage seemed, much like her current life, rather confining. Though she supposed a husband and children would make her less lonely.

She hoped.

Regardless of how she felt about any of it, she would do her duty to Mathav. Her mother had died in childbirth, trying to give the King a son who would rule. Instead, her father had been left with a girl he hadn't known what to do with, and without the heart to remarry and produce more heirs. A girl who had become an *emotional* outburst of an adolescent and needed to be sent away.

Elsebet tried not to dwell on that now. She had her island, her small measure of freedom, and the promise she would do her duty to her family name and to her country someday. She would certainly never let his devotion to the mother she'd never known be punished by not being exactly what he needed. Now that she was grown, she fully understood this.

It would be a failure and betrayal to entertain any other ideas.

She just wished her duty didn't include being *stuck* here, waiting to marry a stranger her father hadn't even chosen yet. All politics and power and no *love*.

You have indulged in far too many fairy tales, Elsebet," her father had admonished her when she'd still been naive enough to express her desire for *more* to him. *"Love threatens duty. Love is more pain than it's worth."*

She knew her father spoke from his own experience, having lost his wife and feeling incapable of putting duty before her memory. But if Elsebet's life was destined to be nothing more than isolation and duty, why not find enjoyment where she could?

On a sigh, she kicked another rock. The ocean was angry today, the wind was cold. She looked at the castle with its rustic, ancient stones, built to weather just this…and it had, for centuries. Here on this tiny island—the castle towers taking up most of the land—the stones had survived everything the ocean could throw at it.

She was part of that, and she would remain. Her father told her this should fill her with pride, with purpose. She tried to feel all those things. Sometimes, when the castle withstood particularly violent storms, she did. Proud that she was from a long line of Thores who had survived these harsh lands and led their people with strength and courage.

Today, she could not find that sense of pride. Restlessness was the only thing inside of her, no matter how she tried to force it away. She wished she could be the ocean, angry and dramatic. Beating against the boundaries the land tried to keep it in.

On a frown, Elsebet turned toward the sea. The lashing waves. The gray, angry skies. Sometimes she dreamed of wading out there, to see what was beyond the dangerous, rocky cove. Was there a calm sea? More islands? Something like adventure?

It was certain death, so she didn't *actually* consider doing it, but sometimes she daydreamed she was brave enough to find out for certain.

Today, she was only brave enough to walk out

onto the rocks and sand of shore, but still out of the reach of the angry surf, in search of something that might have washed ashore that she could collect to turn into art. It was her only outlet here on this tiny island. Turning ocean wreckage into something beautiful. Dramatic or dreary. Angry or sad.

But only for her.

While dreaming of where each piece of debris or shell might have come from. What a world beyond this small slice of it might look like, feel like.

As she walked, she heard something strange. Not just the howling wind, not the usual crashing surf, but a kind of…*squelch*. A *thud* that spoke of great movement.

Surely she was hearing things on this loud, lonely morning. But still she moved toward the direction she thought she heard the sound. There was an odd little pile of wreckage behind one large boulder. Some wood, a few twisted pieces of shiny metal and then a hint of fabric.

As she got closer she realized the fabric wasn't just debris. It was a man's clothes. *On* a man. Not just a human who happened to be *male*, but a large and muscled figure, curled in a kind of heap. His clothes were torn, and his head and arm were bloody. But he was most definitely a *man*.

He moved, and just the twitch of his arm produced an odd, sucking sound in the sand. Elsebet jumped back, startled, but then quickly rushed forward. She had no idea how this man had washed up on her isolated beach, where no one dared sail. Perhaps she should have been more cautious approaching him, but it was clear he was hurt.

She knelt next to him, the damp from the cold sand seeping into her dress. Gingerly, she reached out and touched a cheek that wasn't bloody but was far too cold. "Come. Wake up."

Dark eyelashes fluttered, then she was pinned by nearly black eyes that met hers. She could see pain. And confusion. But he breathed. He lived. Her heart thundered in her chest, but she smiled.

"There, there. I've found you," she soothed. "We'll take care of you just fine."

Danil Laurentius never allowed himself to be caught off guard. He was not his king's most trusted guard simply because King Aras of Gintaras was his half brother. Danil was trusted because he was the best. Because he would give his life for his half brother, and the small nation Aras ruled. Danil was strong, ruthless, cunning and *never* at a disadvantage.

He had built himself into a legend, and had never once faltered. Because this was what Aras required, and Danil owed his brother *everything*.

These were all things he remembered, with some clarity. How he got to be on this beach, aching and confused…this he was not clear about. Particularly when dark blue eyes the color of an angry ocean looked at him with a sweetness incongruous with anything angry.

He half believed her to be a siren. He *had* been sailing, hadn't he? He cast back in his memory for some answer. He had been sailing one of his smaller boats, but…why? Where? Had she lured him to the rocks? Would she drown him now?

He was just addled enough to wonder if it was even worth trying to escape someone so beautiful.

Foolish thought, that. He stared at the woman— blonde, slight and dressed in a plain frock that nipped in at the waist. Her long hair was pulled back, but many tendrils had escaped in the harsh wind and blew around her face. She wore sturdy boots that looked like they might keep out the wet and cold.

She had a fragile air about her, but she knelt next to him as if she didn't feel the cold at all. Something about her was oddly familiar and this gave him the errant thought to reach out and touch her wind-whipped cheek.

It would be warm, and he was very, *very* cold.

Her mouth curved, and she said something, but he didn't quite catch it in the rushing wind.

This all felt like little more than a dream. He blinked, wondering if he could dislodge her. Maybe she was a hallucination.

He tried to say something, but at the attempt everything inside of him erupted in a fire of pain. He moved, but that too started a cascade of new agony through him. So much so he could not clarify the jumble of his thoughts. If this was a dream, it was a nightmare.

Except for her.

"Stay here and I will get help," she said, louder now. Her voice was oddly accented, and she did not speak his native tongue, but it was still a language he knew.

But could not think of the name of it.

Well, this was not good.

She stood as if to leave him here. And though he'd *heard* her mention help, the thought of being left alone filled him with a dread he did not understand.

He was *often* alone. It was how he lived his life. How he *preferred* things. All the better to turn himself into the invincible machine that would protect his brother at all costs. The legend of Danil Laurentius, King's Guard, fierce and fearsome warrior and commander of a navy he'd built up himself and a troop of Aras's soldiers, whom he'd spent his adult life training.

The Weapon.

But the thought of losing this little bright spot in the midst of a howling wind had him reaching out, in spite of the pain that shot through him. His hand curled around her forearm before she could stand and move away.

She was so warm. He needed…something.

Her eyes widened at his grip, but she did not wrench her arm away as he'd half expected. Her eyes softened even more and she knelt again. "Oh, you poor thing." She swept a hand over his brow, but it came away bloody. She tsked. "I can't possibly move you to the castle myself. You must let me go get you some help. I promise, it will be quick. And we will take good care of you, sir. You need help, and quickly."

He knew he must have a head injury, because his instinct was to believe her when he knew better than to trust random strangers on an empty beach. No matter how pretty she was or how sweet her voice.

Ignoring all the pain in his body, he moved, forcing himself into a sitting position. All the while she tutted at him and told him not to. He ignored her and fought off her attempts to keep him still.

His head throbbed. It was like excruciating fire to breathe, to swallow. And still he did not let himself rest. He used a rock to leverage himself onto his feet. He fought off the dizziness with every last shred of strength he could manage.

"You shouldn't be doing this," the woman continued to scold, as if he'd ever listened to a scold in his life outside of his grandmother's kitchen, and even that had been lifetimes ago.

The siren moved to his side at once, pressing her insubstantial frame to him as if he should lean on her, when his size and weight would no doubt crush her.

Though he didn't dare lean too heavily, the warmth of her and the way she stood upright while the world around him spun helped him find his footing. And not pitch back to the sand. He felt something thick and wet slide down his forehead, then his cheek.

It landed with a *plop* on the tip of his frayed boot. Blood.

"Well. You're up. So we'll get you inside and warm at once. Nielson will take a look at you. He's a doctor, so you needn't worry. We'll stitch up what needs stitching. Get you warm and fed and then figure out how to get you home. Are you alone?"

He opened his mouth to tell her he'd never had use for a doctor in his entire life. He cleaned up his own scrapes and broken bones, *thank you*. But it hurt, and no sound would come from his mouth.

As for being alone…he couldn't remember just yet. He looked out at the sea. Angry and stormy. Yes, he'd been alone, hadn't he? On the small boat he'd built years back. But why would he have sailed that small boat into such a place as this?

He shook his head.

"Your throat looks very bruised," she said, those soft eyes of hers looking anguished as she encouraged him to step forward with her. "It would likely be best if you didn't try to speak until Nielson has checked you over."

Danil pressed his lips together. He had no desire for someone to check him over, but it seemed *impossible* to speak. Not just because of the pain. He had pushed through all manner of physical pain and torture. Something was *wrong*.

Well, he was half-naked, frozen and injured. So *many* things were wrong. But the woman was leading him away from the rocks and sea and toward a building.

No, not anything as simple as a building.

It was a castle. Narrow though it was, it reached up in brooding, looming towers. Despite its small size when compared with his brother's castle, it took up almost the entire island—because the island was very small. He could see the ocean on every side.

Not just a tiny island, but minuscule. Taken up mostly by castle. With a surrounding rocky beach dangerous and precarious to any sailor who would be stupid enough to try and outsmart them.

Add the pretty, kind blonde currently leading him to the castle, away from the ocean and what likely had been meant to be his death.

Castle. Island. Rocks. *Princess*.

He wasn't sure everything came together then, but he remembered how he'd gotten here. And why.

His gaze moved to the woman at his side. Beautiful. *Royal*. No matter how simply she was dressed, how kind her eyes were. She was not just any random woman.

She was Princess Elsebet Thore. Who was meant to marry his brother. Her father had broken his agreement with Danil's brother, but King Aras of Gintaras would not be denied by a change of heart.

So Aras had sent Danil to this no-name island, this isolated castle protected by only its rocky shores and dangerous coast, with one simple goal: kidnap the Princess and bring her home to Gintaras.

CHAPTER TWO

ELSEBET KNEW THIS was not right. The man should have remained sitting and allowed her to bring Nielson to him. He dripped blood as they walked, but she supposed the fact he walked at all was promising.

She had a million questions to ask him, but there was significant bruising and swelling all over his face, neck and chest—where clearly at some point whatever coat or shirt he'd been wearing had been ripped clean of him. His pants were torn and frayed but remained mostly intact, but his boots were falling apart as they walked.

Blood continued to trickle from gashes to his head and side. It made her heart hurt that anyone could be so injured.

She walked next to him, trying to be some kind of support though he seemed determined not to lean his weight on her. There were a million things she wanted to say, but she pressed her mouth shut. Clearly he needed medical attention before she peppered him with questions.

Though there were so many.

What is your name?
Where are you from?
How did you end up here?
How does one become quite so...muscular?

It was wrong to notice his muscles, the sheer *breadth* of him, when he was in such obvious distress.

Well, no, that wasn't fair. Despite the bruises and the blood and the slow, pained walk, the man did not radiate *distress*. He seemed quite contained for someone who had to be frozen through and injured beyond anything she'd ever seen. Each step had to be excruciating, but he never faltered or made a sound.

All the while, his bare chest kept drawing her attention.

Because he had to be so *cold*. Not because she was fascinated by the ridges of muscles and marks of old scars mixed with new injuries.

They made it to the castle door and Elsebet hesitated. The door was heavy and she was afraid to stop being the anchor he led himself by. But he reached out and, though he made no sound, she knew he was in pain so she stepped away from him and took the heavy door before he could, pulling it open and ushering him inside.

"Nielson?" she called out, knowing he was likely in the kitchen and her voice would carry in the narrow, tall towers even if he was somewhere else.

"Is something amiss, Prin—?" He stepped out and stopped short, his mouth falling open. "What...?"

"This poor man was on the beach. He needs medical attention."

"Win, bring my medical bag. Inga? Bring us some sheets. Old sheets." Nielson shouted, calling for the remaining staff.

"What's happened?" Win asked, rushing out of the kitchen as well. Just like Nielson, she stopped short, though her eyes took a tour of the impressive form of the man standing next to Elsebet. "Oh, my."

"My bag, Win," Nielson said disapprovingly, already stepping forward, his stern doctor-face in place.

When he'd sent her here, her father had been insistent the "head of the castle" be a man who could take care of things, so he'd chosen Nielson. Nielson had been the King's doctor in Mathav, and since coming to the island had taken on the added roles of main communicator with the King and Elsebet's advisor, along with a million other small jobs that kept the castle running—and Elsebet safe and healthy.

But not happy.

She shoved that thought away as Nielson instructed her to lead the man into the cozy living area, where a fire snapped and crackled in the hearth and warmed the room. Inga hurried in with sheets and Nielson instructed her to put them on the couch.

After a few bustling minutes, they got the injured man to lie down on the covered couch while Elsebet and Win washed out his injuries and Inga threaded a needle per Nielson's directions.

Elsebet had never dealt with much blood or injury before, so she assisted Nielson with a kind of gruesome fascination. He stitched up the deep cuts on the man's body, instructed the rest of them to bandage others after they'd been cleaned. He tutted over the bruises and told Win to get some painkillers and ice.

The stranger winced as he swallowed the pills down but was otherwise perfectly stoic as Nielson ran competent hands over the rest of him, checking for other injuries.

The man did not speak, but he'd nod or shake his head as he answered the Nielson's questions.

Elsebet knew she *shouldn't*, but she couldn't help but wonder what it might feel like if *she* was the one running her hands over this man's body.

"We have stitched you up and bandaged you, sir," Nielson said. "You have some severe bruising and swelling at your throat. I would recommend not trying to speak for a few days to allow the swelling to subside, and some of the bruises to heal. We will do what we can to make arrangements to have you transported to a hospital, but this will take some time as we are quite isolated."

The man shook his head. A clear refusal of the hospital.

Nielson's eyebrows drew together. "You'll need more help than I can offer."

The man's dark eyes moved from Nielson and met Elsebet's gaze. He shook his head once again. He clearly wanted her to refuse *for* him.

Elsebet did not know why she felt honor bound to do so, only that she did. She turned to Nielson, who often capitulated to what she wanted.

Except when it came to her safety.

"Nielson, surely we don't need to worry about hospitals if the man could walk himself into the castle?"

"It is not for you to say," Nielson said firmly.

But Elsebet knew how to get around his firmness. While Inga and Win fluttered around the injured man, putting a blanket over him and whatnot, Elsebet drew Nielson aside, far away enough the man wouldn't be able to hear their conversation.

"He's conscious and able to understand what's happening. He just needs some rest," she suggested.

"I can only examine him from the outside. He could have internal injuries. It is a danger to the man to keep him here."

Elsebet looked over at the large, uncompromising form on the couch. It was hard to believe anything about him was *in* danger.

"The idea of a hospital seems to distress him. If he takes a turn for the worse, we can worry about transporting him to the mainland then."

Nielson's frown was stern and disapproving. "This is quite irregular, Princess."

Elsebet nodded. "It is, but he walked in here of his own accord. He doesn't want a hospital. Let's give him a few days to recover, then reevaluate." Nielson was always a fan of waiting and reevaluating when it came to *her*.

Nielson frowned deeper. "The King would not approve."

"Father doesn't need to know."

"Elsebet."

He only used her first name when he was *deeply*

disapproving. But Elsebet knew what would happen if they told her father about any of this. And so did Nielson.

Elsebet tried not to let emotion seep into her voice. She did not wish to hurt Nielson's feelings or have him withdrawing. So she kept her gentle smile in careful place. "He would not allow me to leave the castle. I would be under lock and key once again. Nielson." Her voice threatened to waver, but she could not let it. "I cannot go back to that."

Nielson sighed heavily, a sure sign he would give in to her. In some ways, he was more a father to her than her own, no matter how unfair it was. But Nielson was always here. She only saw her father in person a handful of times a year. Less if she was particularly *emotional* during his visits.

This man had nursed her through illnesses, eaten breakfasts with her, tutored her in math and science. He'd continued her lessons on her responsibility and duties as a royal. He'd taught her how to identify the shells on the beach and dried her tears when she faltered and he saw her sadness.

She loved him as a father, and she was quite sure that he loved her as a daughter, though they never said those words. She smiled brightly at him, knowing she could get what she wanted because he *did* care for her. Her freedom. "It will only be our secret until we can decide how to get him home. He's simply a wayward sailor. There is no threat here."

Nielson's face hardened at that. "That man is not *simply* anything."

Elsebet looked over her shoulder at the man currently dwarfing the couch. Even with the bandages, his bruises were visible. Even under the blanket Win had settled over him, it was clear he was…

Dangerous.

No, not that, of course. Just very…big and strong.

And what was wrong with that?

"Only until he gets his voice back, Elsebet," Nielson said, clearly trying very hard to sound fierce. "Then he must go."

After some time spent whispering and eyeing Danil warily, the small group found him clothes that apparently belonged to this Nielson person, and made quick alterations to let out seams and hems to fit his much larger body.

Danil was fed some flavorful broth that he could not enjoy due to the pain in his throat—even after the painkillers. Then Nielson and one of the maids, Win, informed him that he would stay on the couch through the night as there were no bedrooms on the main level and he was clearly not well enough to climb stairs.

Danil was fine with the arrangements, as it left him close enough to the door should he require escape. The Princess was kind—too kind—but her staff was far more mistrustful of him.

He respected them for it.

His two biggest challenges at the moment were his injuries and the fact he'd lost his ship in the storm he now remembered. Fierce, sudden and inexorable.

When he'd been *so* close. But he did not count this as a failure. He was here and alive, wasn't he?

He would need his voice to make arrangements to get another ship though, as he could not risk any communication that could be found or traced. There could be no evidence of what he needed to do prior to him doing it.

He would need to get a little stronger to accomplish what he'd come for anyway. He wouldn't call himself *weak* by any means, but the injuries had definitely slowed him down, and likely would for a few more days.

The Princess would be easy enough to kidnap. Her dedicated and suspicious staff of one old man and two women were certainly no match for Danil, even weakened by his injuries.

All that soft kindness in Elsebet made her the perfect mark, if not a perfect queen. But that was his brother's problem. Not Danil's.

The true challenge would be getting another ship into and out of the dangerous cove. He had been the only one brave enough to sail it in the first place. Finding someone in his brother's employ who could bring him a ship safely, without meeting the same fate or worse, would be a problem. And even if they could do it, Danil would need his strength at a hundred percent to make certain he could get Elsebet out.

He pushed the blanket off now that he'd been left alone. Lying about would not help him any. He would only get stiff and find himself in more pain. He needed to stay mobile. Stay *ready*.

A weapon was always prepared.

But before he could get to his feet, the Princess swept in. She had changed, though her new dress was as bland and serviceable as the last. It showed off an hourglass figure that would no doubt look beautiful in silks and jewels. She might be too soft to be a good queen for Gintaras, but she would certainly *look* the part.

She'd refastened her hair so few tendrils spilled out, but the wavy golden mass of it fell down her back. No doubt as soft and silky as it looked. And those dark blue eyes, all warmth and liveliness. Yes, she could be a siren, no doubt.

But she was not dressed like a princess, nor did she fully act like one. She fit in well with the servants and had no qualms about seeing to him. Something that should be far beneath her notice.

Perhaps they did things quite differently in Mathav.

"You must rest, sir," she greeted with just the hint of admonition in her warm tone.

She was a princess and yet she called him *sir*. It was quite strange. Danil was not royal himself—a king's bastard who had been raised in poverty, then found out and saved from his sadistic biological father by his brother, the true heir, who had not concerned himself with legitimacy but given Danil a place in his guard.

So, no, Danil was nothing royal, but he was *around* royalty all the time as his brother's guard. He knew the way they acted and thought.

Except Princess Elsebet did not act like any of the

royals he knew. Aras would not be caught dead in drab attire. The women of Aras's court would *never* lower themselves to take care of an injured man on the beach. Danil could not help but think Elsebet would have quite a struggle ahead of her when she became the Queen of Gintaras.

But, again, that was not his problem.

Elsebet held a notebook under her arm and dragged a chair over to where he sat on the couch. She settled herself on the chair, only a few inches away from him. They were alone in this cozy little room, a fire crackling in the middle of it while the wind lashed the small, recessed windows that dotted the stone walls.

This would have never been acceptable back home. A princess and a commoner alone in a room? Insanity.

"Nielson is quite adamant you should not try to speak," Elsebet said, holding out a notebook and pencil. "But that doesn't mean we shouldn't try to communicate. How lonely it would be for you to sit here in silence with no company."

Danil studied the outstretched items, then the Princess's delicate face. No one had ever been concerned about his *loneliness*, least of all him. He should be suspicious of it, but she only smiled, and he found himself…feeling something odd. Something he could not find a name for. A wanting…to speak to her.

Luckily, he could not.

"It would be much easier if there was a name I could call you by," she said, pushing the paper and writing utensil at him.

He slowly took the pad of paper in his lap, the pencil in his hand. She wanted his name.

The name Danil Laurentius would likely mean nothing to her, but it might mean something to her father. Then again, outside of his brother's kingdom, he was usually only referred to as *The Weapon*. The more faceless and nameless he was, the better for his missions, he had always believed.

But it was always good to leave a bit of a calling card. It was good that people knew all he was capable of. They would *fear* him and all he could do in service to his brother.

No one else could have survived the storm Danil had just come through. No one else could have gotten as close to the rocky cove as he had successfully— before the gale had swept up, angry and bitter and with no warning.

No *man* was match for him, but Danil had a healthy respect for the screaming, deadly pride of Mother Nature, a woman to the last. Once again, she had bested him.

But she had not won.

He was here. Where he'd meant to be. Bloodied and bruised, but alive. Once he recovered his voice, made arrangements to get a ship, he would take the Princess and return to Gintaras, only a few days later than planned.

Danil would not be thwarted. Such was his confidence that he scrawled his actual name on the paper. *Danil*.

He left *Laurentius* out of it for now. Perhaps once

he succeeded in taking the Princess to his brother, it would be a kind of clever calling card. Far, far too late for her meager staff to do anything about it.

"Danil," she said, and it was strange. Something about her accent, or the gentleness she spoke with, imbued his name with a softness that reminded him of a sunny, cramped kitchen in his grandparents' home—such an old memory he thought he'd erased.

So few people used his name these days, but even when they did, it was with the same ferocity they called him *The Weapon*.

Because that was what he was.

The Princess beamed at him and something inside of him shifted. Uneasy and foreign. A kind of warmth when he was from a cold, cruel country. *Proudly.*

"Where are you from, Danil?" she asked pleasantly. "Is there someone we can contact for you? Surely someone out there is worried for you? Family? Parents?" She looked down at her lap, then up at him through her golden lashes. "A wife, perhaps?"

Danil did not raise an eyebrow, though he wanted to. She had all the hallmarks of an innocent, and even if she had not, it was quite well known in the royal circles his brother frequented that Princess Elsebet had been isolated here in this tiny castle as a youth, hidden from the world while her father shopped her about. His virginal princess sacrifice meant to save his pitiful country.

Perhaps her father did not know everything if she was bold enough to be questioning Danil about his marital status. He *had* noticed her gaze on his body, more than once. And yes, she was meant for his brother, but Danil was no stranger to using a woman's reaction to him to get what was required.

So he smiled at her. Slowly. Darkly. Until a faint hint of pink crept up her elegant throat and into her cheeks.

If her reaction caused a stirring of his own, he ignored it. He took his pleasures in the appropriate places befitting his station. His lack of heart and soul. With women who understood.

Not soft virginal princesses who blushed and were meant for his brother.

But it was a surprise how hard he had to fight that reaction away. He focused on writing, though his arm throbbed with a dull pain, even after the pills he'd been given. He used the pain to control himself.

I am from nowhere and have no one.

It was a bit dramatic, but sometimes a flair for drama suited the situation.

And intrigued a woman.

Kidnapping was so much easier when a woman was intrigued. So he showed her his response with another silky smile and ignored his own leaping response to the way the flush on her cheeks deepened.

CHAPTER THREE

ELSEBET TRIED NOT to fidget, though strange sensations fluttered through her. Made her cheeks heat. Something deep and likely shameful throbbed within her.

But the way Danil smiled at her was like sin itself, all the adventure she craved promised in his dark brows, high cheekbones and sensuous mouth.

He looked no less dangerous covered in Nielson's altered sweater. The bruising, stitches and bandages on his face only added to the undercurrent of threat. And yet she was drawn to it like moth to the flame.

"I'm very sorry to hear that," she managed, though her voice did not sound like her own but instead a strangled kind of thing.

He shrugged as if it was no consequence to be from nowhere and have no one. When to her...well, it sounded worse than what little she had. Because perhaps she'd never had freedom or choice, but she had Nielson, Win and Inga. She had her father, sort of. She had this castle and this beach. Her birthright—even if it involved marrying a stranger.

She studied Danil once more. Because he too was

a stranger. Obviously not one her father would ever allow her to marry, nor one that she would *want* to, since she knew next to nothing about him. Just that… actually coming into contact with a stranger put her father's plans for her in a new light.

She had always considered it a boring kind of duty. Say *I do*. Unite two kingdoms. Have children. Hopefully find a better balance with her father if he could see her as her own woman and not just the ghost of her mother. But she had never considered it in more than those sort of fuzzy, fairy-tale images.

Danil made *a stranger* seem…dangerous. Would her future husband be so big and strong and…*essential*? Would he make her stomach tie in knots with a simple, wordless stare? Would she *pulse* every time he smiled at her just like that?

Her father had long since bemoaned her obsession with *questions*, and she bemoaned herself in this moment. None of these questions were helpful—answers or no.

She cleared her throat, straightened in her chair and affixed the smile her tutors back on Mathav had insisted she learn. Kind but bland. Warm but not an *offer* of warmth. "*You must seem approachable but remote.*"

That hadn't made much sense as a child, but it did now. Putting some kind of barrier between her and Danil seemed…necessary for her very survival. It helped her every day when her wayward emotions got to be "too much."

"How did you arrive here, Danil from nowhere and no one?"

He wrote once more, with short, sharp strokes.

I am a sailor. I suppose I got turned around.

He held the notebook toward her, and that same dangerous smile flashed on his face, but Elsebet was not quite *that* naive. She saw it for the lie it was, because she could not imagine this man had ever gotten *turned around* a day in his life.

"There isn't much this way to be heading for," she said, as if genuinely confused rather than suspicious. "You must have had some goal though? Some end destination in mind out there on the ocean?"

He looked down at the paper, paused, then wrote very carefully.

The details are a little...fuzzy.

He waved a hand around his face as if to demonstrate *fuzzy*.

Elsebet did not narrow her eyes at him, but she wanted to. Turned around and fuzzy? She didn't think so.

It was hard to believe a man this injured could wash up on her beach and be some kind of direct threat to her…but this *particular* man did not give off *accidental* vibes. She simply couldn't believe he'd ever landed somewhere he didn't want to, no more than she believed he didn't remember every last detail he wished to.

His eyes watched everything with an intensity that spoke of filing every detail away. The way he moved, even seated on a couch in borrowed clothes, was with confidence and a sense of ownership—even injured, even in a castle decidedly not his.

And there was simply *no* reason any sailor's ship should be close enough to this isolated island to be *turned around* and washed up to shore. So there had to be something he was hiding.

Elsebet could not decide if it was narcissistic or simply *smart* to wonder if his secret had something to do with *her*. After all, her father had ensconced her on this island for her "protection." Just because that safety had never been breached before didn't mean it couldn't be now.

No doubt Nielson was right, and letting this man stay here while he recovered without telling her father was dangerous, but…

Letting her father in on her suspicions would result in her having even fewer freedoms than she did now. The thought made her entire body feel weighted with a heavy depression she could not fathom living through.

She had so little already. How could she give up more?

She would simply have to be careful. Watch Danil. Be smart about it. Because she would not give up her freedom.

Even if it put her in danger.

And what kind of danger might this man offer?

She should be afraid. Worried. Instead, all she could seem to think about was what an *adventure* that might be.

Win's voice rang out from the kitchen. "Dinner!"

Nielson had cautioned Danil against any difficult-to-swallow food while his throat healed, but no doubt Win had put together some more broth or something soft for him. So Elsebet smiled his way.

"Ah, dinner." She stood. She couldn't say she was hungry. The insides of her body were too busy doing acrobatics. But it was a good distraction. Besides, regardless of his injuries, he needed to eat and keep his impressive strength up.

But he did not stand or make any move. So she held out her hand. "Come. You must eat with us. You're our guest."

He studied her, then her hand. A silence stretched out that swept around them. She felt darkly compelled to close the distance between them, though she did not move. She just stood, a few feet away, her hand extended.

He took his time. Moving. Standing. She told herself it was because he was hurt, but the slow unfurling of his body seemed to make that *thing* throb deeper inside of her. As he towered above, so tall, so large. His eyes so dark and so intent on her.

His slid his hand into hers and her breath caught. It was rough, large, strong. It was a simple touch, casual even, but a thread of heat poured into her body, wound through her limbs, until it felt like everything around her was gone. And there was only him and her and where they touched.

She didn't breathe. He did not speak.

Because he cannot, Elsebet, she reminded herself

harshly. And still she did not look away from the dark depths of his eyes.

Maybe she was drowning.

He nodded, a sign he was ready to move into the kitchen.

A sign you should stop being such a ridiculous ninny.

So she finally dragged her gaze away, though it felt as physically demanding as trying to move boulders at the beach. She didn't pull her hand away from his because that would appear like some kind of weakness.

And she knew what she looked like, sounded like. She knew there was great weakness in her, but she also knew she was a princess. A Thore.

She would not give in to her weaknesses quite so easily. She would *not* wear them on her sleeve any more than she had to.

She let out a shaky breath and tried to find some inner peace and strength. Held her head high as she led Danil into the kitchen for dinner.

Because he might be dangerous, but she was no shrinking violet. Not when it mattered.

Danil found himself beyond confused by the situation in this castle. The Princess ate with the staff. They all came together, shoving elbow to elbow around a small table filled with plates and bowls and food that looked and smelled delicious and hearty.

It reminded him, fondly, of eating in the mess on one of his larger ships with his crew when they were off on a mission for his brother. Certainly not of the stifling, formal dinners he was sometimes forced to attend with his brother at the royal court as personal guard.

But Elsebet was a *princess*, and none of this was befitting royalty. Maybe his brother had the wrong of it when it came to Elsebet and what she might offer Gintaras. Maybe the Kingdom of Mathav was very poor and would offer Aras next to nothing. After all, no princess of Gintaras would eat in such a humble setting.

And speaking of princesses, the one seated to his right was an interesting puzzle. She was clearly innocent, naive, not guarded when she should be. He had seen the reactions chase over her face—when he smiled at her, when he placed his hand over hers. These were not the blushes, shudders or breath catches of a sophisticated, worldly woman.

And yet there were little moments when they'd spoken before dinner, where she'd looked at him just a tad askance, and Danil had wondered if she saw through him.

Then her expression of distrust would be gone, and her warm smile or blushes would replace it.

Since *no one* saw through him, he supposed he was imagining it. It paid to be careful, after all. But she was a kind, soft little isolated princess and she could not know what he had in store for her. There was no need to worry.

Food was doled out family-style, though Danil had been cautioned by Nielson to stick with things that would not irritate his injured, swollen throat. And

Danil noted there were quite a few options on the table that were soft, like Win had very kindly made things just for him.

He did not know what to do with this possibility, so he did not dwell on it. He took what food would not be pure agony on his throat and set about eating, because he would indeed need his strength.

Conversation around him was very casual. He was quite certain his brother would have termed it *gauche*. The staff spoke of what items the pantry was running low on, what damage the storm had done to the castle, and how they would repair it.

But it wasn't just the staff who spoke of such things. The Princess was also part of the conversation. As though she *worked*.

"I'll handle the tower window," she said, after they'd discussed a crack in one of the panes. And there were no gasps or horror, no looks of censure. Everyone nodded as if it was typical for the Princess to do menial repairs.

"Nielson is *terrified* of heights," Win supplied, giving Danil a kind of conspiratorial smile.

"Oh, come now. *Terrified* is an exaggeration," Elsebet corrected kindly. "The tower *is* quite high, and it can be a bit intimidating if you're afraid of falling."

"And our Elsebet isn't afraid at all," Inga said. "She even once tried to climb down the outside, Rapunzel-style, just to see if it was possible!"

Danil slid a glance at Elsebet, wondering what her reaction to this story would be. But she smiled into her cup as they continued on about this childish prank. That, if he was pressed, he supposed he could admit required *some* bravery.

Foolish though that bravery might have been. Usually all true courage started with foolish bravery.

Not his, of course. His had been born of having absolutely nothing to lose. Much like Win had said of Elsebet. He was not afraid of falling at all.

He'd already seen life at its worst.

"Then there she was, hanging from the balcony," Win continued. "Nielson practically a puddle of nerves on the ground." Everyone laughed, even poor Nielson.

Danil would have joined them if it didn't cause such pain, and he did not know the last time he had ever been prompted to laugh at something quite so… tame. But he smiled kindly, because it seemed there was little else to do with all of them shoved together like poor commoners.

"I simply don't know what else Father expected me to do, installing me in this fairy-tale castle, cut off from everything. It's truly a miracle I haven't tried to build my own boat and sail away."

"Come now, Princess," Nielson said, his voice warm and fond, further confusing Danil about how this country treated its royalty. "Don't pretend you haven't attempted to build a boat."

Elsebet laughed at that, clearly pleased to her toes, though Danil couldn't understand why such impertinence would make *anyone* at this table laugh.

No, he did not understand this little group of people or the country they came from.

"Danil is a sailor," Elsebet said to the table. "I was asking him questions and having him write down answers for me."

"Elsebet. The man was nearly killed," Inga said with a tsk. "Your questions are enough to fell a fully healthy man."

Again this censure did not cause anger or hurt or even a hush to fall over the room—as any complaint about his brother's behavior would have caused back in Gintaras—resulting in either angry outbursts or, worse, icy silences that would lead to punishments.

"I'm a curious woman," Elsebet replied, and her gaze slid to his. The curve of her smile had been warm and friendly, but when her midnight blue gaze met his, something changed. Sharpened.

He might have called it sultry if he thought she *meant* it to be. But he was quite convinced whatever changed in Elsebet's smile was completely unknown to her.

Still, it didn't matter. His body reacted. Much like when he'd put his hand over hers. Everything inside of him that he usually controlled to every last twitch had involuntarily leaped to life. He was very injured, and a dull, constant kind of pain gnawed at every cell of his body, and still his blood heated.

She looked away, that faint pink creeping into the apples of her cheeks, and still he stared at her. Not because he couldn't look away—he was *The Weapon* after all—but because he would force himself to look and *not* heat, harden or react in any way.

The goal was to make *her* weak. Not him.

Never him.

So he watched her take a sip from her cup. Her lips perched on the glass, full and pink. The way her throat moved when she swallowed. How she dropped one hand to her lap...and fisted it there, as if she felt his gaze. Deep within.

Underneath the hazy pain he was accustomed to beat a lust that took him off guard, and it could not win.

But maybe he needed another day of recovery yet. He looked away from her and took another spoonful of his broth, ignoring the heavily disapproving gaze of Nielson. And the highly *approving* gaze of Inga.

Neither served him well. It was best if no one thought very much of him at all.

Except Elsebet.

He glanced at her again. As if she *felt* his gaze, she stilled. Curled her fingers in her lap into a fist once more. Was she imagining his gaze as some kind of caress? Would she be as soft as she looked? Would she smell like the kitchens or the sea? Would she taste...

Well, he would be doing no tasting as she was meant for Aras. So.

At the end of the meal, inexplicably, Elsebet helped clear dishes. Like common staff. Maybe this was all a mistake and she wasn't a true princess at all.

He supposed it didn't matter. He would take her to his brother and let Aras determine how to move forward from there. By that time, Danil should have his voice back and would be able to express his concerns with his brother.

But first, he had to complete his mission. He stood, moving to help clear the table, but Win tsked at him. "It's very kind of you to want to chip in, but you are our guest and injured. You must rest."

He held out his hands as if to prove he didn't need rest, because look how strong and capable he was, but Win only shook her head.

"Elsebet? Why don't you take Danil back to the couch. Maybe find him something to read."

Danil frowned. He did not *do* rest, any more than the royals he knew did anything but. He opened his mouth to speak, but even that hurt and reminded him he should not. So he pressed his lips together.

"Come, Danil. We have many books to keep you company this evening." Elsebet gestured him to exit the kitchen.

He didn't want to. He wanted to prove he was strong enough. Well enough. But Elsebet's staff were looking at him as though they would fight him off from bringing even one dish to the sink.

So he sighed, then gave them all a polite bow and turned to leave the kitchen. Elsebet followed him, and when he glanced back at her, he watched the direction of her gaze. Down the length of his body.

"I'm a curious woman," she'd said at dinner. He wondered how deep she would allow that curiosity to go if she was willing to scale castles and build boats to escape this tiny place.

Which was not for him to know. Ever.

She walked over to a bookcase and dragged her fingertips over the spines. "There's much to choose from."

He frowned at her. He had no wish to read. What he really wanted to do was attempt to build himself a boat. To complete his mission. To speak so he could make a phone call to his brother, who no doubt thought him dead.

Which caught him sideways. If everyone thought he was dead, if he could slip away into a different life...

But of course that was foolish. He owed his brother everything. He could hardly repay Aras's generosity and loyalty with desertion.

So he put that thought away, the same place where he put any curiosity over what Elsebet might taste like.

"I'm a curious woman."

It was possible those words would haunt him.

"Here. Try this one," she said, pulling a book off the shelf and handing it to him. "Sit. Rest." She pointed at the couch.

He took the book but looked at the couch without sitting down. He did not wish to be confined. He needed to move this restless feeling out of him.

"Well. Good night," she said, somewhat stiffly and suddenly. She turned to leave, but...

A good sailor acted on instinct quickly. He moved without always knowing why or what he intended. He let that instinct guide him because he knew the ship, the ocean, and how to survive them.

Reaching out and taking her arm before she could leave was like hoisting the sail at exactly the right time. Some kind of innate knowing, the move accomplished before he'd even thought it through.

She looked down at where his fingers curled around her bicep. Then up at him. "Did you need something?" she asked, and he could hear how hard she tried to sound *royal* then. A kind of blandness mixed with just the very hint of disdain.

It made him smile. But he could not speak. Could not say anything as incendiary as he wanted to.

This was a blessing, in the moment.

He tossed the book on the couch and shook his head. A clear sign he did not want to read. He pointed at the door. Then mimed walking with two fingers.

"You wish to take a walk?"

He nodded. Then pointed at her.

"With me?"

He nodded once more, not letting go of her arm. It was all in a bid to soften her to him. So that when it came time to escape, it would be easy enough to do. He would not *seduce* her.

He would not need to.

"I do usually walk the beaches every evening after dinner, but…" She hesitated. "You should rest. Read or sleep or…rest."

He shook his head.

Elsebet looked back at the kitchen, no doubt wondering if her little staff would approve.

But no, he realized. She *knew* they wouldn't approve. She was wondering if she could get away with it.

Then she took his hand off her arm but did not take the moment to escape. Instead, she threaded her fingers with his and hurried them both toward the door.

CHAPTER FOUR

NIELSON WOULD NOT approve of her walking unchaperoned with Danil. She was risking him making a call to her father, she knew. Nielson was more on *her* side than her father's, but he had no desire to see her compromised or in danger.

Surely everyone saw the danger in Danil even if Elsebet wasn't totally certain what that danger was.

And yet the opportunity, even if it promised freedom for only a few minutes, was far too tempting to ignore. Like scaling the castle walls and building a boat that would never be seaworthy. Sometimes there was only so much suffocation she could take before she needed a gasp of fresh air.

She no longer threw tantrums. She didn't yell or cry in front of anyone. None of those things had ever been well received or fair, so she'd let them go. But there were certain…pressure valves that needed opening sometimes. And in this moment, Danil felt like one of those. Cold and wild and *necessary*, if only in this small moment before she was passed off to some stranger to be a wife.

"You will save Mathav, Elsebet," she heard in her father's stern voice. *"And you will not be burned by love."*

So she dropped Danil's hand and rushed ahead, away from her father's voice and her own duty.

She was very aware that Danil's injuries kept him in a kind of…cage. No doubt once he was healed one of his strides would make up two of hers, even if she ran. No doubt nothing would stop him then from whatever it was he sought.

A shiver ran through her. She knew it should be fear, but it wasn't.

Still, though he walked with a precision she did not think was natural to him, he did not fall behind. They made it to the beach and both simply stopped and stood there at the edge, between scrubby grass and rocks and sand, and watched the ocean beat angrily against the shore.

The weather had not calmed any since this morning, but instead of gray the skies were a wild kind of orange, glowing eerily from behind the thin clouds. It wasn't stormy weather—likely they'd wake up to a clear beach tomorrow—but it was as if the storm from last night was holding on to the sky by a thread, not quite ready to give up its grip on the cove.

Elsebet glanced at Danil. Something about the idea of storms and calm necessitated seeing his face, his expression, and what his dark eyes looked like when he beheld the sea.

She saw something in him, something she recognized on a soul level: that gasp of fresh air she'd needed. His eyes tracked a wave far out in the dusk, as though he'd held himself into a million tiny compartments inside the castle but here on the beach he could let go.

Expand.

If she were alone, she would climb to the top of a boulder, spread her arms wide and fling her head back, letting the icy wind move over her and through her—a reminder that no matter how tiny and inconsequential and isolated she felt, there was a wild world out there. Somewhere.

Even if she never got a slice of it.

But standing with Danil on this beach felt similar anyway, so there was no need to embarrass herself.

She eyed him as he studied the misty, narrow entrance to the cove. She did not think embarrassment would be what she felt with his eyes on her. Ever.

Oh, this was dangerous. She heard all the warnings she'd always been taught whisper in her mind. But here on the beach, she was free. She could do as she pleased.

Before she could decide what that was, Danil began to walk down the length of the beach. His stride was careful but certain as he made a beeline to where she'd found him, curled in a heap in the rocks.

How *had* he survived?

Occasionally he paused, toed something with the boots that Inga had attempted to mend since nothing they had would fit him. He seemed to have a destination in mind, so Elsebet trailed after him, watching the way his body moved. For a large man, an injured man, he was incredibly graceful. Like some sort of large, feline predator.

Another shiver ran through her that she *wished* was from the cold, but she had more self-awareness than that.

She hadn't paid much attention to his surroundings when she'd found him—she'd been too concerned with the blood.

And his chest.

She shoved that thought away. When they reached the spot where she'd discovered him, she found little evidence he'd ever been here. The wind and surf had washed away any indentations, any trails of blood. It was just sand and debris once more. Broken boards and sticks and other flotsam and jetsam from the ocean.

But she paid more attention to the boards. They weren't what she would normally salvage for her art, because these were very big and straightforward. She preferred putting the small and delicate together to make something fearsome and pretend it was her.

Danil's brow furrowed as he stared at the spot. Perhaps the planks were the debris of his own ship? Because while she did not believe he'd been turned around or didn't remember, she did believe he had to have been a sailor to wash up here so injured. No matter *why*, surely he hadn't meant to do that.

He certainly hadn't inflicted those bruises and gashes on himself.

"Was it yours?" she asked gently as he stared.

He knelt carefully. No doubt the movement hurt,

but he didn't stop. He picked up one of the broken planks and turned it over in his hand. Then he gave a simple, curt nod. She could not say she saw emotion cross over his face, but there was something about the way he held the single piece of splintered wood that made her heart twist.

She had often heard that sailors loved their ships like wives or children, and his had been splintered into pieces. While he had barely survived. There must be *some* kind of grief in that. She was too accustomed to grief not to want to offer some solace.

She stepped forward, placed her hand on his shoulder in some thought to comfort. Because she could not imagine what he'd seen. What fear must have swept through him. Surely he'd imagined he might die. He could have, if she had not found him. If he'd swept up on some deserted isle.

It weighed heavily on her. That anyone could simply be swept to sea and…be lost. That someone like Danil, so large and full of…mystery and wild *otherness* to her, might have simply been killed by the conscienceless whims of Mother Nature.

"I am sorry such a thing happened to you," she said solemnly.

For a moment, he crouched there, perfectly still. Then slowly, he turned his head to look up at her. Confusion knit his brows together, but he smoothed it out as he straightened, unfurling to that great height. She had to tilt her head back to hold his gaze.

She moved onto a rock, so she felt less like she was being intimidated by a giant, though she still had to incline her head back to meet his gaze. But this move also put her closer to him. So there were mere inches between her chest and his. The wind whipped around them like a vortex, but she felt warmth in the midst of all this cold.

He was wild and unknown, nothing she could ever really have. *Dangerous*.

But, oh, how she wanted something wild and unknown. Just a little slice. Just *once*. Something of her own that no one—not her father, Nielson, or the Kingdom of Mathav—had any say in. Something outside of the life that kept her in a very careful box.

She wanted to scale the castle walls, sail the ocean in a boat she'd built. She wanted to press her lips to this unknown man and see what it might be to taste danger.

So that was what she allowed herself to do. Reach to her toes on the rock, curl her hand around his neck and kiss him.

The kiss was timid. Danil could see the pulse scrambling in Elsebet's neck, feel the tremor in her hand on his neck before she even pressed that soft, innocent mouth to his.

He did not stop her, as that would not get him what he wanted. What he *needed*, actually, as his wants had nothing to do with this mission.

Danil watched her as she squeezed her eyes shut and pressed herself to him with more enthusiasm than skill. It was clear she did not know what she was doing.

But he did.

And *knowing,* he should be careful. He'd certainly always been careful and calculated before in everything he did, but all that seemed to desert him for a moment. Because the warmth of Elsebet's slender body pressed to him felt like sunlight on his face after sailing through nothing but clouds for weeks on end.

Before he'd thought the motion through, he lifted a hand and tested his fingers against the soft skin of her cheek, her jaw, angling her head to soften her lips against his. To run his tongue across the seam of her mouth.

To taste.

He had a purpose here, a reason for doing things, or so he thought. Then her mouth parted on a little surprised inhale, granting him a deeper access he shouldn't take but in the moment craved more than his next breath.

Because she tasted like the *sea.* Crisp and promising. Deep and dark underneath the pretty, sparkling surface. It was meant to be a bit of a lark. See exactly what she might offer, how he could use this surprising turn of events to complete his mission.

But the water was closing in over his head. Her kiss was potent, surprising, not what he'd prepared himself for. His body throbbed with the pain he'd felt since waking on the beach, but desire twined through it, turning it into one formidable feeling he did not recognize. Her hands clutched his shirt as she pressed herself closer. And his arms came around her waist, holding her securely on that little rock she was perched on to give herself some height.

His fingers spread wide, spanning her waist. So slim, so delicate. But her mouth was eager, hot, willing. The pang she drew out of him was sharp and old, something he'd thought he'd eradicated as he'd turned himself into *The Weapon*.

A tool. Heartless and soulless. More machine than man, needing no one and nothing. A kiss was a kiss meant to lead to sex and nothing more.

But this was…not that. She was…

Innocent.

Meant for your brother.

It was this reminder that brought him back to who he was. *The Weapon*. He did not jerk away. He had to be smarter than that. He eased her instead, lingering another second or two at simply the gentle brush of lips. When he finally pulled his mouth free, he focused on the pain in his throat, in his arm, in his head rather than the sweet softness of Elsebet or the warm bubble she'd encased them in.

He stared down at her, trying to put his thoughts back into their proper order. Trying to ignore the demands of lust his own body seemed intent on satisfying while her blue eyes swirled like a tantalizing, tranquil sea…that no doubt hid dangerous reefs and icebergs.

Elsebet was not his to have. A few smiles, even some kisses —these could all be forgiven as a means to an end, but that was all his brother would forgive. Elsebet was meant to be Aras's, and Aras did not share.

Still, Danil stared down at her. Because she had been the one to initiate an act she clearly didn't know much about.

Why had she done such a thing?

She did not scramble away as he half expected, though her expression was arrested. Perhaps she was terrified frozen since she wasn't blinking.

"Did I hurt you?" she asked on a soft whisper, concern clouding her eyes. But her fingers were still clutched in his shirt, like she didn't know how to let him go.

He might have laughed if his throat did not scream at him. This little slip of a princess hurting him? He didn't think so.

He shook his head, brushing a hand over the wind in her hair, ignoring an old shift in his chest that ventured too close to a tenderness he no longer had nor believed in.

She *was* a siren, innocent though she was, but he would not be felled. He could not reject her out of hand. It would create an emotional response in her that would make his eventual kidnapping attempt more difficult. A woman scorned and all that.

But he needed to tread carefully.

"I am sorry such a thing happened to you." She had said this to him with such genuine empathy there in the wreckage of his ship.

As if she truly was sorry. As if it mattered to her. When that storm and shipwreck and *this* were some of the easiest challenges he'd ever faced. He'd lived, hadn't he? That was all that mattered. Survival.

He sucked in a deep breath of cold air, painful though it was. He needed to think more clearly, and no doubt being alone with her on this moody beach heading toward dark would not do much for *clarity*. Because dark creeping in only tempted him to think of the things they could do in the dark. Where no one could see.

Where no one needed to know.

And this could not be. She would soon be his queen. Never his lover. Though his hardened body demanded other eventualities. But he was the master of himself. Always.

He took her hand in his. Small but not soft. Not like a princess's hands should be. Because she washed dishes and baked bread and scaled castle walls, apparently.

He was going to have to recalculate. His initial plan had been the element of surprise. Sweep in, take her, sweep out. But now he was beginning to see the story of her.

A woman locked away in isolation. Maybe not unhappy, but restless. Restless enough to kiss a stranger, clearly not knowing what she was getting herself into. Desperate for some freedom.

She would not get freedom in Gintaras, but she didn't know that. Nor did she need to. She only needed to want to escape *this* prison before she worried about the next.

So he could offer her that escape. Once the time

was right. He helped her off the rock and then began walking them back toward the castle. She mounted no objections, but she kept her hand in his as they walked. As if they were innocent lovers taking a sunset stroll. He might have laughed to if he'd been able at such a ridiculous thought if he'd been able.

When they reached the castle, he felt her hesitation. He was leading her back to her prison. No matter how good that prison was, how nice her jailors were, Elsebet clearly wanted a taste of the unknown. Danger. *Freedom.*

He knew this desire well enough to recognize it on anyone. And he would use it for his own means.

She made a move to open the door, but he stopped her. He lifted her hand and brushed his mouth across her knuckles, gaze meeting hers in the faint glow the castle windows offered. He even smiled and tried to make it soft. Then he reached out himself, ignoring the stiffness and pain in his arm, and opened the door for her.

She looked up at him through her lashes before she moved inside, under his arm. She gave him one last look over her shoulder, then strode inside to where her staff was already speaking to her. And frowning at him suspiciously.

But Danil only smiled, attempting to make himself look smaller than he was. He wasn't a threat. He was simply a shipwrecked sailor rendered dazzled by their beautiful princess. Who would not be?

He would turn himself into a fairy tale they *all* wanted to believe in. For Elsebet, the miracle that might help her escape her isolation. For her staff, simply a nice, innocent sailor in puppy love with her.

And alone, where the staff could not hear, he would make Elsebet promises of the world out there so when the time came, she would join him easily, willingly.

He would offer her all she clearly wanted—badly enough to inexpertly kiss a stranger on a beach. Adventure. Romance. He could be the castle she scaled, or at least thought she did. Perhaps she was more dangerous to his control than he had counted on, but he was *The Weapon*.

She wouldn't even realize it was a kidnapping until it was too late.

CHAPTER FIVE

ELSEBET'S MIND WAS a scramble, but she smiled and nodded and spoke with Nielson and Win as if everything was just fine. Yes, she'd gone for her regular evening walk and Danil had joined her. No, nothing was amiss.

She did not miss Nielson's disapproval, but she held on to the hope that his concern would not outweigh his sympathy over her isolation.

And he could *never* ever know she'd kissed the man. Kissed. She wanted to laugh. That word did *not* do what had happened out on the beach justice.

Inga handled everything to help Danil get ready for bed, and Elsebet was ushered away. Up and into her tower.

A prisoner.

She tried to push that thought away. It was unkind and untrue. Everyone wanted what was best for her and Mathav. She was hardly treated poorly. She had nothing to complain about. Nothing to be upset over. That never did any good.

She tried very hard to convince herself of that,

but all she could think about was the way she'd felt when Danil's arms had spanned her waist. Like an entire new world had opened up for her. Wild and unknown. Something with no plan, no walls, no *cage*. Just a soaring feeling of being *free*.

And no matter how she tried to convince herself she might feel the same with *any* man, with the man her father chose even, she had a hard time believing that feeling was *ordinary*. That it was generic to kissing, and not specific to Danil himself.

He'd kissed her and she'd felt like *his*, like they were two interlocking pieces that belonged together. Always.

Too many fairy tales, Elsebet.

"You should not be alone with him," Nielson said grimly as Elsebet swept into her room, hoping to leave Nielson and Win behind.

"A walk on the beach is hardly being alone." She crossed her room to her window seat, where her little turret window looked out over the cove. The one place she felt free.

And Danil had kissed her there, as if she was. She resisted the urge to touch her fingers to her lips that still tingled like a kiss could be magic.

"He could have hurt you or forced you into any number of terrible things out there!" Win cried, then looked over her shoulder, clearly worried Danil might have heard her shout all the way down the stairs.

"And then what?" Elsebet returned, very calmly. "There's nowhere for him to go. He can't even speak.

I understand the desire to be cautious, I really do. But Danil isn't a threat." She knew this was a lie.

She did not care.

He'd kissed her. She was sure she was supposed to be…shamed somehow. But she had initiated it, she had *thoroughly* enjoyed it, and she wasn't so foolish to throw away her entire kingdom just because she had.

Sometimes, a taste could be enough.

She was going to try very hard to believe that.

"Elsebet. I am warning you. Even a hint of untoward behavior will *have* to be reported to your father. I know you crave more than this isolation, and I understand it. I feel as though I've been very lenient," Nielson said with a restrained kind of anger Elsebet knew spoke of fear. Of her father's disapproval. "Perhaps *too* lenient."

Elsebet looked away from the window and to Nielson, who had indeed always been lenient. She knew that he loved her like a daughter, that he gave her as much as he could. She never questioned it. And she didn't now.

She only questioned if his love for her was more important than her father's will. Which would win out? What she wanted, desired, perhaps even needed—or what her father did?

Still, she smiled at Nielson in an effort to soothe. They did not need to carry the weight of her feelings. "It was a walk. He can't even talk. It's simply me babbling on and him being forced to listen. Just like you lot. We found a bit of the wreckage of his boat, and I feel that might have been cathartic for him."

"We like listening to you, Princess," Win said loyally.

"And I appreciate you all. Along with your concern. But there is nothing to be concerned about here. I'm sure Danil will be eager to leave in a day or two, once he's recovered a bit more and can contact someone from his homeland. He does not seem like the kind of man content to haunt a castle on a tiny, isolated island. Does he?"

Nielson and Win exchanged a look. Elsebet knew they agreed with her on that point, but there was something more in that look that she couldn't read, and she could only blame it on her inexperience.

Which did not help with the frustrated feeling swirling through her. The desire to do something reckless and *more* that might free her from…

What? Your duty? The one thing you've promised to uphold?

"We only want what's best, Princess," Nielson said softly.

Elsebet nodded and smiled and did her best not to let her eyes fill with tears. Unfortunately, just because some people who cared about her did their best did not mean this felt tenable. How long could she go on, getting older and more alone? "I don't suppose Father has given any estimated time of when he might pick my husband?" Which she didn't want, but she didn't know how long she could keep *waiting*.

Nielson shook his head. "I could check with him again, Your Highness."

"No, there is no need. He will make the decision when it's best for Mathav, and that's what's important." She smiled brightly at them, or at least tried to. "Now, I'm very tired after the excitement of the day. I'll bid you both good-night."

Nielson bowed, Win curtseyed, and they left her with soft *Sleep wells*. For a moment, Elsebet only stood in her little room perfectly still. She had endured the loneliness this long, the heavy weight of it, the dark, spiraling frustration of it. She could keep surviving it.

After all, she'd done something today that she'd never done before. She'd kissed a man. He'd kissed her back. Her first kiss. And not just a *kiss*. His hands had been on her body. She had *tasted* his mouth.

It had been wild, like the waves crashing into the cove. It had been the promise of something bigger out in the world than she'd ever imagined, and oh, had she *imagined*.

The way his fingers had spread wide. The strength inside of him, the sound he'd made when his tongue had touched hers. A kind of *growl*, when she'd never heard him say anything due to his injuries.

Elsebet was very sheltered, this she knew. But knowing it meant she'd also endeavored to be slightly less sheltered. She read whatever she could that might give some glimpse into what happened between a man and woman. What might be expected of her on a personal level when she was married off to some stranger to uphold her duty, her family line.

She liked to think she'd been *somewhat* educated by her curiosity, and tonight had given a new glimpse into *all* of that.

She was very grateful for fiction. It allowed her to at least *understand* the pulse between her legs. She had read enough to fantasize about what it might be like, to have a man touch her in all the places she was meant to keep *pure* for her future husband.

But now the fantasy man had a face. Large hands. Scars. And dark, piercing eyes. A man who could never be her husband.

And was that really so terrible? She couldn't have real adventure, real danger, which Danil seemed to embody on a cellular level. Her duty would never allow it.

But maybe she could have the fantasy. A kiss. A daydream. It didn't have to be *real* danger. It was relatively safe, all in all.

But when she dreamed that night, nothing about Danil or his hands, or his mouth, was *safe*.

As the days passed, Danil tried to not think he was being imprisoned. He was a patient man, laying the groundwork and all that. He smiled. He helped with chores. He played the role of meek, humble sailor gone astray—a role he had long trotted out when it served him.

As a large man, as the King's bastard whom for years only Aras had trusted, Danil had learned how to make himself look smaller, kinder. While also learning how to use his size, his temper to intimidate and terrify when necessary.

If he was being honest with himself, intimidate and terrify was much easier. But as long as his injured throat kept him from speaking, there was no way out of this with intimidation.

No doubt everyone back home thought he was dead. There would be no ships waiting for him outside the cove—he'd been the only one brave enough to attempt it in the first place. So he needed a few more days to get his voice back, and then he could make contact with someone in Gintaras to get a ship sent to him. Give specific orders on how to make that happen, and whom he trusted enough to bring one of his ships here.

Danil could not let this opportunity slip out of his fingers. It would be a failure, and that was not tolerated. By Aras or Danil himself. Because Aras had once saved him, and Danil could not betray his brother with failure.

When his father had wanted him killed for being the blight he was—an unsanctioned bastard who dared be a son, older than Aras by two days—it was Aras who had interceded.

This would not have been needed, of course, if his mother's husband hadn't gotten wind of his true parentage and thought it some kind of get-out-of-poverty-free card. Trying to claim the crown for Danil had been foolish on every level. As if the King would have ever let him be heir. As if Danil *wanted* such a thing.

So the man who'd married his mother after his grandparents had died was sentenced right along with him. *This* at least was justice. Frick had died in prison. Danil had been saved by Aras, who had asked only fidelity in return.

Danil owed his brother so many things it did not do to count them all. So he would not. He would bring Aras Elsebet, his chosen bride. Failure would break all those old, dungeon promises.

It would be the end of their brotherhood.

And it was clear after a few days that Elsebet would be a fine enough queen for Aras. At first Danil had only seen her softness, but she had a kindness, a cunning way about her in how she dealt with people—him, her staff that she treated more like family—that Aras critically needed. To smooth out his rough edges, his impetuousness. That rage of temper that so often got Aras, and the Kingdom, into trouble. Trouble Danil often had to clean up.

If it settled uncomfortably that Elsebet would have to deal with such things, it did not signify. If it felt wrong to put that kind of responsibility on her shoulders, he needed to lose those feelings, the way Aras had endeavored to beat them out of him.

It was not *The Weapon*'s job to have opinions, thoughts, or feelings. It was his job to be his brother's tool.

A position that had come to him out of his brother's generosity. Of his own doing over time, because he liked being that machine that had no feelings to be betrayed by, the kind he had struggled with as a child.

His mother's broken promises after his grandparents had died. The man she'd married, who had "known better" than her. Who would make him into a "man." He had invaded their home, and his mother hadn't just let him, she'd *welcomed* him. Allowed him to parade Danil up to the vicious king, knowing full well what would happen. There'd been a reason she'd kept that secret all those years prior, hadn't there been?

The old anger swirled through him, bitter and ugly. And utterly useless. So he froze them out, as he had learned to do from his brother.

Better to be a weapon.

It didn't matter how blue Elsebet's eyes were, how her smile unfurled inside of him like sunlight. That she asked him questions as if those thoughts, opinions and feelings *did* matter. That she had welcomed him into her family—as had all of them, no matter how suspicious—and made it easy to feel *belonging*.

When there was none to be had. He was *The Weapon*. She was Aras's prize.

Never his.

Every day that passed, Danil was grateful to her eagle-eyed staff that they never let Elsebet alone with him. He could have gotten around this of course, but he was biding his time. Letting Elsebet set the rules, test the limits. Being the perfect guest to her staff.

And not letting himself get too tied up in Elsebet. A minute-by-minute struggle he had never counted on.

Because despite the fact there were always eyes on them, Elsebet did not act all that differently. Oh, there were no kisses, but she talked to him as if it was just the two of them. Tales of her most favorite finds washed up on the beach. Why she enjoyed making bread. What she thought existed beyond the cove—

a mix of practicality and fantasy he found himself drawn to.

Making her more and more real to him, when it was better to think of her as a prize to be won and handed over to his brother.

She talked about her art until he was curious enough to write out the words *May I see it?* Mostly because it seemed to be secret, and the more secrets he knew the better chance he had of kidnapping her without her knowing it.

Or so he told himself. He certainly couldn't allow it to be actual curiosity.

He had no curiosity left. He had seen everything. The bleak, the bad, the terrible. Freedom, all the blues of the ocean, and many beautiful women, who had been more than eager for a bit of rough.

And yet he could not recall ever feeling the way he had when Elsebet's lips had been on his. As if despite how little they knew about each other, their souls were made to connect.

He willed these thoughts away as Elsebet seemed to mull over whether she would show him her art.

"I have a little studio of sorts, but it requires many stairs as it's up in the tower."

He nodded, a signal he could handle it. Though much of his body still ached, most of his injuries had been sustained from the chest up. Not only was he capable of mounting many stairs, he *wanted* the exercise. He hated feeling so pent up and useless.

He hated even more the idea of putting that feeling to pen and paper. So he simply gestured at the stairs. She glanced at the kitchen, where they both knew Win was half listening to their conversation.

Then she stood. "Well, I shall take your leave for a bit. I'll be back for tea." But instead of leaving the room, she walked toward him. Leaning close so the sweet smell of vanilla enveloped him.

Her lips at his ear, sending sensations through him that should have warned him this was a very bad idea. "Wait until Win starts humming. Then quietly come up the stairs. Just keep going until you can't go any more. I'll be there."

She straightened and then walked away, and he watched her go. The braid down her back, the soft, unconscious sway of her hips. She didn't look back, not even once. But she would wait for him, he knew.

It was strange to feel as though he stood on the cusp of danger. Like facing down a tidal wave in his tiny ship. His body hard and wanting.

I'll be there.

He shook his head. It was ridiculous to let his injuries affect him like this. To consider a little slip of a woman a danger when he had faced down monsters. He was stronger, savvier than some innocent. No matter what kind of siren she was.

He always had control in any situation. Desire, lust, yearning, these were no match for an iron will forged in honest-to-goodness dungeons, his life on the line. He would use this *attraction* between them to get what his brother wanted.

But only that.

So he sat where he was until he heard the soft

strains of Win humming from the kitchen. Then he got to his feet, and though there was something beating at him to hurry, he took his time.

Just to prove he could.

The stairs seemed to go on forever, twisting in a constant spiral all the way up into the height of the tower. It was almost dizzying, and this too he blamed on his injuries.

But she waited for him at the top of the stairs, that soft smile on her lips. Mischief and excitement in her blue eyes.

Siren.

And you are The Weapon.

"Follow me," she whispered, as if there was anywhere else to go when he reached the top. They passed a closed door as they curved around the tower to the other side. She led him into a room with an open door. The walls were stone and it might have been dark and dingy, but there was a series of windows—ovals, squares, circles, diamonds—all around the rounded walls. They let in little shafts of light. But most of the light came from the domed ceiling made of stained glass. He looked up, considering the marvel that all this glass could act as a ceiling.

Surely it wasn't very practical. But it was stunning. Two sides spiraling together—either in fight or embrace—sun on one side, moon and stars on the other.

"It's so high up, and the glass so thick and carefully arranged, we've never had any damage to it," Elsebet offered as if reading his thoughts.

He looked from the ceiling to her, and how she

stood in the middle of the room, all that colored light settling over her like a mask. They stood there, silent and staring at one another, for too long.

She was the one to break his gaze, gesturing around the room at the tables that were set up at places where the light was best. Projects littered the tables, even clustered along the curved wall.

He might have considered it little more than the arts and crafts of a child, but the end result of her work was all over the room.

It was all…astonishingly beautiful. He was no art expert, but Aras had quite the collection of art—antique and modern—and these pieces would easily fit among those famous ones.

There was a little corner where the projects were more rudimentary, dark and angrier, and it said something about her—something he wished he didn't see—that she hadn't gotten rid of those early attempts.

She had it all. A clear progression from furious, clumsier adolescent to graceful, understanding woman. He did not look at her but perused her art instead. Most of them were mosaics of sorts, made up of beach flotsam and jetsam cobbled together in interesting ways. There were a few paintings, some driftwood carved into interesting shapes. Some of it was abstract. Like emotions swirling to life in vibrant colors and interesting shapes. He could not put to words what those made him feel.

"I've always wanted to sail out to sea where you can't see land," she said as he stared at one that was blues, grays and shocking bolts of yellow. "To be un-tethered. Free." She pointed at the mosaic. "I suppose that's my best guess."

He could not speak, but it was…not a guess. It was as if she'd been there before. Even though it was ab-stract, it reminded him of exactly what she described. Boat in the middle of the ocean. Just him and water and sky and sparking light. So beautiful it could make even *The Weapon* sigh.

He nodded at her, trying to make it clear that her best guess was correct. Her beaming smile in re-sponse was like the sun shining through the window. Warm and bright. He wanted to bask in it for eternity.

But he had a sailor's sense of danger and forced himself to look away. To not let himself be blinded by anything that might be too good to be true. Any-thing that was not *his*.

And she was not. No matter how that art piece settled inside of him like belonging. Understanding. Things he had not felt, warm and comforting, since he'd been a small boy, fishing from the pier on his grandfather's knee.

He shook these memories away. What was she doing to *him*? This was supposed to be about getting her to trust him. To want him. So she would come with him.

He moved away from the abstract pieces to the largest piece dominating the bigger portion of one wall. It depicted a sprawling castle, not unlike his brother's, though the world around this castle was sunny. There was a colorful village in the background, bright churches, villagers on the streets and beams of light in the blue sky. It was made out of bits of seashell and glass. It had to have taken an incredible amount of time and patience to put it together.

"That is Mathav," she said, standing a good few yards away from him. He half wondered if she was afraid of being close. "My home. Well, before I was sent here. Though I like here better. Mostly."

It was the mostly that poked at him. The tool he would use to get her away from her kind staff. Her family. That feeling of *mostly*.

Because anyone who was *mostly* happy was tugged at by something that made them unhappy. A thread they couldn't stop tugging at.

You should know.

He frowned a little. He had snipped all his threads. He was not unhappy, because he was nothing. He was a weapon, that was all. And this reprieve of recovery had no bearing on the choices he would make.

Once he had his voice, a ship, he would take her—willing or not—to his brother. She would be the Queen of Gintaras.

And Danil would need to somehow scrub from his memory all he had already filed away.

Like how her eyes changed color with the sun. Or what her laugh sounded like. Now he knew what she could create with that fascinating mind and her own two hands.

He knew what she tasted like, and this most of all haunted him every night.

Elsebet was getting to be a *problem* that wasn't so easy to shove away, no matter how strong he was.

"I guess you can't tell me what you think," she said, with a sweet little laugh that swirled around inside his chest as if he had a heart that beat there. "But you aren't frowning, so I'll take that as a good sign."

He nodded. Once. There was no way to express how impressed he was with simple hand gestures, and that was likely for the best. As would getting out of here be.

"It has helped fill my time anyway," she said, her gaze traveling back to the mosaic castle. "Back home, there was not much more to do. My father has always been very protective. So it's not like I was out roaming the streets."

He looked at the streets in question. The pretty shops. The way the sun glistened on them in her artistic depiction. He could feel the yearning.

Knew all too well the yearning. Their prisons had been very different—hers protection, his an actual dungeon—but he knew what it was to look out a window and see a world you could not be part of.

Well, she would have…some freedom in Gintaras. Sort of. Aras could be somewhat…overbearing to the women in his life, but Elsebet would be different. She would be his wife. The Queen. She would have to be seen. She would have to have duties.

She laughed a little. "I was such a little hellion it's a wonder he kept me around as long as he did."

He frowned at this, shook his head. Though he could see the passionate side to her, *hellion* seemed incongruous to the sweet, kind woman who'd taken such good care of him.

"You don't believe me?" She shook her head, and he could see her try to laugh it off, smile about it like she'd left childish rebellion behind, but there was a sadness in everything she said. "The more he tried to protect me, the more I chafed. The more I yelled or cried or made myself a nuisance. Really, he had no quarter but to send me away. For my own good."

Again Danil shook his head. There was no *good* from being sent away. He knew this. Maybe he'd been more like taken away when his mother's husband had taken him to the King, but still he knew what it felt like to be ripped from that which you loved.

Loved. He had loved his childhood home, and his mother, and then Frick had poisoned it. Because love was far too fragile a thing to survive *life*. He reached for Elsebet, without thinking the move through. Because he was driven by emotion. By feeling.

When he wasn't supposed to have any of that left inside of him. *Stop this at once*, he ordered himself. He smiled and gave her hand a kind squeeze, because he needed her to trust him.

Then he dropped her hand and stepped back.

"Is it what you expected?" she asked brightly, purposefully turning away from the mural. She was smiling at him, but he saw the sadness in her eyes. Like she was trying very hard to be *bright* when she felt anything but.

He nodded again, knowing it would be best to find another piece of art to focus on, or perhaps return downstairs. But his feet were planted, and the air around them glittered with colorful sunbeams.

She looked like a fairy tale brought to life, and if he believed in fairy tales, he was the villain. At *best*.

But she moved toward him, studying him just as she had on the beach. With curiosity. Interest. She even reached out, placed her small hand over his heart. She had nothing to stand on here, so there was only their height difference between them. And he realized that he'd bent his head, without ever meaning to.

When every moment since he'd been an adult had been purposeful.

"Danil," she whispered as her hands slid up his chest, burning through him like fire. Overtaking him like a wave. His name in her accent, her soft, sweet voice. It pierced him clean through and it was in that *feeling* he wasn't allowed to have, didn't *want*, that he found the strength to step back.

"I cannot." It was a rasp, barely audible, and it hurt like the devil. But there it was. His voice. His truth.

Another taste of her might ruin him.

But over the thrumming of his heart, the roar in his veins of wants thwarted, he dimly realized she had *also* said something in that moment when his traitorous voice had come back to him.

And it had sounded a lot like *I cannot*.

CHAPTER SIX

ELSEBET'S HEART BEAT so hard she thought she was vibrating. She'd wanted to kiss him again. Resisting had nothing to do with what she *actually* wanted. Which was his mouth on hers.

No, that was a lie, and she should not fool herself in this moment.

She'd wanted far more than a kiss. She wanted to know what his hands on her body would feel like, without any of her clothes on. She wanted to taste him. More than just his mouth. She wanted all those things she had never experienced, and she wanted them with Danil.

She had not been raised to believe in fairy tales, even if she had always found happiness inside their pages. Her father had always and only spoken of duty, responsibility, the Kingdom. Not of love or contentment or joy—he had so clearly cut those things off when her mother had died.

So she had always known she shouldn't believe the stories she read. That she should think of adventure and love and pleasure as nothing more than fiction.

It had been easy to believe when she'd been virtually alone. When it was only her and the sea and her little surrogate family.

But it was harder to believe that there weren't a million experiences out there, just beyond her reach, now that Danil had arrived. It now felt like adventure must be just outside the cove if a man such as Danil stood before her.

She did not know this man. She might *feel* things because of him, but so much of *who* he was remained a mystery.

But whether she knew him or not didn't matter to this desperate, throbbing electricity that sparked between them. With a look, with a touch.

How could she believe duty was superior when she knew he tasted dark and rich and like a million mysteries?

It was physical, yes. Because he'd never spoken until this moment, and even how he'd only spoken two words. Still, these days he'd been here, he'd listened to her. Maybe he didn't have much of a choice, but he always made her feel as if he took every little detail on board, no matter how silly. No matter how she'd just been filling the silences with old stories and childish wishes to remind herself she could not kiss him again.

And always his eyes were on her. Always he nodded. *Always* he at least acted like he understood. She was not a fragile bloom to be protected, an emotional roller coaster to be hidden away. She was someone worthy of company, of *interest*.

She had three people in this castle who cared about her, this she knew. But she had never had the sense any of them *understood* her. Not her yearning or her curiosity or her desire for something beyond duty. They thought that was as childish as her father thought her tears were.

Still, they loved her and she loved them and that made Danil even more dangerous. Because it wasn't just *her* he listened to, spent time with, helped. Danil listened to them as well. He helped without being asked, even when he was told he should rest. He got things off high shelves for Win, carried heavy things for Inga, and even helped Nielson deal with some temperamental light fixtures in the library.

He fit into this little life she had learned to love for its sweetness, its little snatches of freedom. Its family and love. She wished he could stay long enough to speak, for her to get to know him, to make fairy tales a reality.

And now, here in this moment, he'd looked at her art with interest, and she had seen a matching…something in his eyes as she'd spoken of a protective father. She could not explain it. She only knew that he understood something of being held back.

It made no sense, a man of his size, his power. Surely he did and got whatever he wanted.

But he had to understand *yearning*, or that look would not have appeared in his eyes.

In that moment, so quick but so potent, she'd wanted something she yearned for to come true. For a split second, she'd been willing to risk everything for that. Just *once* getting exactly what she wished for. Just like the other night on the beach, pressing her mouth to his.

But it had been her father's castle behind Danil, in mosaic form, that had reminded her of who she was.

What she was.

What she'd promised.

And though she had touched Danil, she had also pulled back.

But so had he. And now Danil stared at her as if she'd spoken a foreign language. Like he couldn't understand *her* resistance, though he had some of his own.

Because *he'd* spoken, too. He'd sounded rough and pained, and whether it was because of how he felt or because of his injuries she could not begin to parse.

I cannot.

Cannot. That word meant something held him back, and the only thing she could think of was… "Oh, so you do have someone waiting for you." It crashed inside of her, dark and horrible. When it didn't matter or shouldn't. He had someone, a woman he'd likely pledged himself to. Kissed, touched, loved.

Why else could he not take what she'd *offered*, no matter how wrongly on her part.

But he shook his head. "I do not," he said, though his expression was one of pain. And the pain got through to her more than anything.

"No, don't speak. It hurts too much." She patted his chest, this time to soothe. "Just because you can doesn't mean you're fully healed. Rest."

He looked down at her, mouth in a grim line, but slowly he raised his hand and put it over hers on his chest. So warm, so large, so rough. The scratches on his hands were healing, but old scars marked his skin.

She should step away from this. It was too much, and her father had always warned her that her many *too much* vices would lead her down the same path he'd walked. Pain. Loss. A dereliction of his sacred duty as a Thore.

For the first time in her life, she thought she understood. That emotions could be dangerous, threatening, even when they *felt* good. For the first time, she was faced with a want that *threatened* something.

And now she knew why she'd been taught that a dutiful princess did not test herself. She kept herself above reproach. She thought of her duty, her promises.

Because she wanted Danil, not a future husband. She wanted to share her body with him, chase these feelings, not save herself as she was meant to. *Danger.*

She knew why she could not, once more, press herself to him. Touch her mouth to his. Why she could not have what her body desired—a pounding need that had become something more than *needy*. There was weakness in *needy*, but she felt nothing weak about this.

It was as strong and vast as the ocean, this feeling swirling inside of her. As demanding as the storm that had brought Danil to her beach.

How could a man who'd spoken only a few words to her sweep inside of her like those things? How could her responsibilities be shaken by a man who'd only showed up and *listened*?

But no, it wasn't *all* him. Because she'd had questions before. Wondered why her duty mattered. But that had always felt vaguely self-pitying. Whiny. Or maybe her father had only made certain she felt that way when she'd complained. Cut her off more and more until there was little left. Of course, Nielson had told her once that the older she got the more she looked like a carbon copy of her mother, and that might explain some of her father's increasing distance as she'd gotten older.

But King Alfred hadn't been completely wrong about her early anger and frustration at being sent here. Her complaints *had* been childish then. Her thoughts had all been about her own feelings and not the Kingdom, because she had been *thirteen*, and she hadn't been able to care about the Kingdom.

But now, as the years had passed, her feelings had become adult. Why did she not get to make the choices? Why was it someone else's decision that she could not kiss this man, learn this man, give herself to this man who brought out so many sensations within her with just a *look*?

She cared for Mathav and her legacy, but why should her father's devotion to her long-gone mother be seen as a failure? Wasn't it *beautiful*? Why did she not get to chase that beauty?

Danil made all her dreams of something else seem real and vibrant and *possible*, instead of the foolish fantasies of a bored little girl reading too many fairy tales.

He represented what else there might be. Because surely whoever her father might pick out for her wouldn't affect her like *this*. Surely this thing that bloomed between them was unique.

Or was it? How would she know?

"I could save you from that which you do not want." His voice was little more than a rasped whisper, but it wound through her like a booming proclamation.

Save.

She should say no. She should adamantly shut this conversation down—she was not really a prisoner, not really in any situation that required *saving*. She had accepted her duty.

But for a moment, fleeting and irresponsible, she could picture a whole different future than she'd ever considered. Somewhere else. Free of kingdoms and duties. In the middle of the ocean, just the two of them. No need to hope for her father's approval, because it would not matter there.

"How?" she whispered, though there was no need to speak so softly.

He shook his head. "Think about what you want, Elsebet."

Elsebet of course could not *think* about it. There was no rescue from what she'd chosen. She had a duty to Mathav. To her father. And maybe it wasn't fair, but it was what mattered.

More so than this man.

But the way he rasped her name lived inside of her now. On repeat, for the next few days, as she considered all that she could not do.

Danil spent the next two days testing the limits of his voice, but only when he was alone and no one could hear. He couldn't speak for long. His vocal cords seemed to stop working at all after a few words. So he waited. He did not want to find the opportunity to call his brother only to be rendered mute after a few words. It was frustrating to have been here over a week, and still not be well enough to set his plan into action.

He did not speak to Elsebet after that moment in the tower. He was not alone with her again.

Even when her gaze felt as heavy as any caress and his body acted in kind. He focused on being the perfect guest. So that when he left here, Elsebet in tow, everyone would be surprised the kind, shipwrecked sailor could do such a thing. He was determined it would be before the next week was out.

Maybe the staff would even create their own fairy tale around it. Nielson seemed too practical and devoted to his king, but the women might sigh over a love story for their princess.

He did not think they were so removed that they did not see the way Elsebet looked at him when she thought no one was paying attention.

Or the way you look at her. He scowled at that thought as he sat around the dinner table. Everyone was cheerfully discussing topics related to the keeping of the castle. Pantry stores, repairs that needed done.

Danil had the strangest thought sneak through. That he might…miss this. The conversation, the warmth, the *hominess*. It tried to remind him of bits and pieces of his childhood he'd long since shoved into the recesses of his mind.

His grandmother's shaky voice and warm breakfast biscuits—better than anything he'd ever eaten at the palace. Mornings on his grandfather's lap, the smell of strong coffee wrapped around them. His mother tucking him into bed before she'd married and soured everything.

How dare these strangers stir up these old memories best left behind? How dare they include him in their little conversations and warm dinners and *care*?

He had no use for this. He did not belong in the midst of *this*. He was *The Weapon*. Whom loss could not hurt. Who would not allow loss to change *everything*, as his grandparents' deaths had.

"Are you in pain, Danil?"

Danil raised his gaze to the concern in Inga's eyes. She blinked once, as if taken aback by the expression on his face.

Which no doubt had been dark and mean as he'd been thinking about Frick and all the spaces he'd swept into after he'd lost his grandparents. All the things he'd ruined simply because his mother had been blinded by grief and stress.

Danil tried to smooth out his expression, along

with everything inside of him. The past didn't matter. He'd left it behind, so he shook his head.

He had not spoken to anyone except Elsebet back in her tower. He did not think she'd informed her staff of his returned voice, and he would also use this in his favor as long as it lasted. It helped him look far meeker than he could ever be and would ideally keep the trio from becoming too curious about him that they might actually look into him. Or tell their king about him.

"If everything is feeling okay," Win said, smiling at him with a mix of kindness and something far more canny in her expression. "A sailor has some knowledge of these repairs, does he not?"

Danil had not been paying attention to the conversation before Inga's question, but he nodded. He used the pen and paper he now always carried with him to write *I would be happy to help.*

"The materials should come in next week," Nielson said, looking Danil over skeptically. Danil did not know what the man was skeptical about, but he could not help but respect the man for his carefulness.

Danil did not plan to be here in a week's time. But he smiled and nodded, nonetheless.

But then Nielson skewered him with a hard look. "However, the ship that brings them could also take you back to Mathav once it drops its cargo, if you are up to the short voyage back. From there, you could return home. Wherever that may be."

There was clear censure in that last sentence. That

he had never told them where that was. That he had let himself remain a mystery.

Danil did not let it poke at him. He took it for what it was. Growing suspicion. But his voice was back, his plans were in place. Suspicion didn't matter because he—and Elsebet—would be gone before Nielson grew the courage to do anything about it.

So Danil took his pen and wrote, before showing the paper to Nielson.

Whose frown only deepened.

I would be happy to take the ship back and return home. My imposition has gone on long enough.

"Oh, you're no imposition," Win said, giving Nielson a hard look. "I'm sure the Princess has enjoyed having someone besides us to keep her company."

Danil smiled at Win's kindness, then slid a look to Elsebet. She was looking down at her plate. She had been less…cheerful since their encounter in her art studio. She still smiled, spoke sweetly, of course. But she was not as chatty. She acted as though something weighed on her.

Which could only mean she was considering his proposition, no matter how vague it had been. No matter how she'd claimed she could not.

After a few moments, as if sensing his eyes on her, she looked up. Their gazes clashed. Like swords in battle. Sparks. Heat. Memory of that kiss on the beach with the cold wind whipping around them. Of the way her eyes had gotten soft as she'd spoken of her home country, with all that *yearning* for things she could not have. Heartbreak over being sent away, thinking it was her fault.

That echoed so deep in his soul he was afraid he would forget who he was.

The Weapon. He broke her gaze, trying to find some triumph in the pink stain on her cheeks. He had fooled her. She would go with him because she *wanted* him.

And he would hand her over to his brother.

The hand he held in his lap curled into a fist.

Inga sighed a little dreamily. Yes, they would weave stories. As long as Elsebet's father questioned *all* the staff, it was possible he would be confused enough by Inga and Win's reports that he wouldn't suspect Danil of working at Aras's behest and *immediately* go after Aras. Hopefully, he would think in stead that Danil had taken Elsebet for himself.

The way that idea sang within him like a symphony was clearly a side effect of his head injury. So he focused on the next steps. Because he knew well enough that nothing would stop her father from coming for her, but Gintaras was a much stronger country militarily than Mathav. There was only so much King Alfred could do. And it was the King's own fault for breaking a deal with Aras anyway.

No one broke their promise to Aras and survived to tell the tale. As his enforcer, Danil should know

But Danil also knew that timing was important. Because who knew how the ocean would treat him once he got Elsebet on a ship. It could take anywhere from three days to a week to sail back to Gintaras, depending on the weather, the type of ship and the number of men Aras sent as crew—likely not many, since everyone was afraid to sail to the cove and large ships could not handle the narrow strait.

So he would need time.

But first he needed a ship to *get* here. Tonight would be the night to arrange that. He would find a way to make a call to his brother.

He helped clean up after dinner, did not fully understand why he enjoyed making Win and Inga tut at him for doing too much. Or proving to Nielson that he was indeed a helpful member of the castle. Or looking at Elsebet until she blushed a deep red.

It was similar to sailing with his crew back in Gintaras when he was commanding the navy somewhere. You became a kind of…family unit.

The idea of *family* often had him withdrawing on his ship, and it had the same effect here. It was just harder to remove himself from the warmth. There was nothing to do when he did. Only silence and the memories he did not wish to relive would plague him if he isolated himself.

But he had plans to make. So he excused himself—silently. He said nothing to Elsebet even when she bade him good-night in the living room while everyone else was in the kitchen. She even paused, and he knew she was giving him a chance to speak, to offer to save her once more, to explain himself in some way.

But he did not.

He had a feeling the more he pressed, the more

she would resist. Because she had a duty too. It was what kept her hesitating, no matter how much she wanted freedom.

She would cave. She would give in to that desire, but only if he did not push until the right moment.

He waited until everyone was asleep, and the castle was dark and peaceful. Until he was absolutely certain there was no way for anyone to be near, to be listening. In the dead of night, with only the sounds of an old castle and the wind outside, he finally found his moment.

He crept through the castle. It hadn't taken much to find out from Win that there was a phone in the library that was rarely used, but always functioning so Nielson could call the King and vice versa.

Which meant Danil would be able to call his brother. And the only way to trace it would be for the King of Mathav to get his hands on the phone records. Which he could do, of course, but it would take time.

Time was all Danil needed.

Danil turned on no lights, having familiarized himself with every piece of furniture, every creak of the floorboard on the way to the library. Once he reached the door, he eased himself into the dark room without needing a light or making a sound.

He found the chair at the desk, sat himself in it, then lifted the phone receiver. It glowed in the dark and he carefully inputted the number to his brother's personal assistant.

It would be a few hours later in Gintaras, and the

number would come in as unknown, but Danil hoped that since it was Olev's private mobile, he would be curious enough to answer.

"Hello?" a deep voice asked suspiciously.

Success. "Olev. It is Danil."

There was a pause. "You don't sound yourself," Olev said, all suspicion.

"Near death will do that to a person, but I managed to survive my shipwreck, and have been nursed back to health by the target. I need a ship." His throat burned as he talked, and it was difficult to enunciate while speaking softly enough he didn't wake anyone.

"But…you were the only one brave enough to sail out there in the first place."

Danil did not groan in frustration. It would only hurt and there was no point. "I need a ship. Before the week is out. On the island. Tell His Majesty."

"Do you have the Princess?"

Danil stared into the dark around him. He was not convinced she would come with him willingly. There was a sense of duty embedded in her that made him wonder if she would be brave enough to buck it.

Would you?

That question settled in him like a thorn wedged deep. The truth was, he did not know. He *had* known.

Before Elsebet.

Now he felt they were both living in a strange place where a duty they'd never questioned had been made tenuous simply by the existence of each other.

But tenuous mattered not. Succeeding in his mission was the only thing that would ever matter.

"Sir, do you have the Princess?" Olev repeated impatiently.

"I will," he growled, the pain a throbbing, aching thing that spread from throat to chest. Surely it was only his injuries causing that pain to settle on his heart. "Send Peet. He will know how to signal me from the cove entrance. By the end of the week." Then, orders given, Danil hung up.

And sat in the dark of the library, wondering what he'd done.

CHAPTER SEVEN

ELSEBET HAD MADE a concerted effort to stay away from Danil following the moment in the tower. Of course, this was difficult when he was at every meal, when he jumped to offer assistance in any of the chores she usually helped Win or Inga with.

Or when Win and Inga seemed *determined* to throw her and Danil together at every opportunity. Like this morning while making bread. Happily and peacefully by herself in the kitchen. Thinking about an upcoming spring rather than isolation and Danil. Or trying to anyway.

Then he'd entered.

For a moment, they'd simply stared at one another. Her hands deep in the large bowl of dough, his eyes tracking over her like they always seemed to. That had her cheeks heating and heart beating triple time.

"Inga said to help," he said, his voice still a rasp though it didn't seem to pain him as much. He didn't speak around Inga or Win or Nielson. He still always had his pad of paper and wrote answers to them.

She wondered why if he *could* speak now, he didn't, but couldn't bring herself to ask.

Getting to know or understand this man any more was a danger to everything she'd promised herself. And her father.

But she could hardly send him away. It didn't make sense. *Or you just want him near even if you know it's wrong.* She frowned down at her dough but gave Danil a little nod. "I'm making bread for the week."

He walked over to the sink and washed his hands. He still studied her as he dried them off on a towel, so she looked down at the large bowl once more. "We have to shape them into loaves and put them in the pans so they can rise one more time. Watch me."

But his hand dipped into her bowl, taking a handful of dough. She frowned over at him, then watched as he expertly crafted a loaf shape and dropped it into one of the waiting pans.

Her mouth dropped open in wonder. Why, they looked better than hers! "Where did you learn to do this?" she demanded.

"My grandmother," he said, precisely taking another ball of dough to shape.

She tried to picture Danil as a young boy with a grandmother teaching him how to shape loaves. She simply couldn't manage it. He was such a *man*, so vital. How could he have ever been a vulnerable child?

It wasn't something she could bear to think about right now. So she focused on her work. They were nearly hip to hip, their elbows sometimes brushing.

It was entirely too domestic. Which was…wonderful. Like he was part of her little family here. Like he could be.

But he was leaving. *He wants to save you.*

From her duty. From her family. From her country. These were not things she needed to be saved from, because she had chosen them.

For the right reasons?

"How is it a princess knows how to bake bread?" he asked. Conversationally.

It seemed a better topic of conversation than the roundabout going on in her head. "I wouldn't have if I had not been sent here. But, if you haven't noticed, there isn't much to do and I was going stir-crazy. And driving Inga and Win to fits with it. So we agreed to let me do some chores around the castle."

"*Let* you," he said, something like a scoff in his tone. "Such a hardship, Princess. Begging to do work most of us are required to do to get by."

She frowned over at him, surprised at what felt like censure in his tone. But there was a smile on his face. Not censure. Teasing.

That Danil could tease was… Well, it was probably her fairy-tale-addled heart that made her think it meant something. Like he had to *care*, to use his voice to tease.

"And I suppose you were slaving over loaves of bread and chores aplenty?"

Stop asking questions, Elsebet.

"More or less. We lived with my grandparents, and

as I got older, their health suffered. It was up to me to do much of the work around the house."

Her heart ached for him. Such responsibility for a little boy. "Do you have any siblings?"

There was a pause. "A brother."

"How different my life might have been with a brother." Her gaze slid to his. She should not let it linger, but it was such a painful thought. If her mother had lived, if she'd had a brother to inherit the throne…

You still would have been a princess. Likely not isolated on an island and therefore unlikely to have ever met this poor sailor your father would never approve of regardless.

This was why her father had warned her against fairy tales. Once you finally realized they were never possible, it only hurt almost as deeply as any actual loss. The next time she saw her father, she would apologize to him. He'd always done his best. Maybe warnings weren't what an eight-year-old needed, but she understood the *point* of them now.

Danil was closer now, but he didn't touch her, and she didn't dare look at him as she shaped her loaf in the pan.

"I never knew my father. Not really," he said. "He left my mother before I was born. I spent much of my life consumed by what-ifs. What would have been different if he'd been involved? If my mother had found a nice man to settle down with instead of the leech she finally did."

She couldn't keep her determination not to look at him when he said that. Couldn't stop the conversation, couldn't stop learning about him. "You didn't like your stepfather?"

Danil's expression was ice-cold. "He was never anything to me. And I was nothing to him." On the *him*, his voice cracked and he began to cough, pain etched over his face. Elsebet rushed to get him a glass of water.

She pushed him onto a stool and insisted he drink. "Don't talk anymore," she said, rubbing his back and watching the color in his face. He wasn't as pale as he had been, but still she worried about him. Nielson had been a doctor, but maybe Danil needed better attention. Better equipment to make certain everything inside was working and healing as it should.

He sipped the water, his cough subsiding. "I am all right," he rasped.

"No more talking," she said again. She set the now-empty glass aside but didn't stop rubbing his back. Until he took her free hand in his. Clasping her small one between his two large ones.

She looked down at him and her heart tripped over itself in all those ways she couldn't allow.

"You are the kindest woman I've known, Elsebet," he said, with such gravity she thought her knees might buckle. And he kissed her hand in a romantic, gallant gesture. The kind she'd dreamed about, knowing her father would never approve of love.

Danil looked down at her hand in his. She should pull it away.

But she did not. Because his dark eyes, grim and serious, were locked with hers.

"I will not ask again. I will not push or beg." His voice got more and more cracked as he spoke and she wanted to tell him to stop, but she knew he wouldn't.

"When it is time for me to leave, I do not wish to leave you behind. I want you to come with me, Elsebet."

He said it so earnestly. Like it was possible.

She began to shake her head, because giving in to her wants was not the duty of a princess. Of her father's daughter.

"Don't refuse," Danil insisted. "Simply...think on it. Don't give me an answer until the time comes."

She could not stand to be around him after that. It made her question everything. It hurt. And all those questions and all that hurt built inside of her like a tempest. She'd thrown herself out of the kitchen and spent the next three days avoiding him at all costs. Even going so far as to feign a cold.

Her only reprieves were her secret walks on the beach when she snuck out the window in the library. She needed the cold air, the exercise. The solitude.

But the walks kept getting longer, more frequent, and still she could not walk away from her thoughts, her jumbled feelings. Whether Danil was in her line of sight or not, she could not push his words from her mind. He had been here for almost two weeks now, and it felt like he'd been here forever. Like she wanted him to be.

She could tell his childhood had been more painful than hers. That he too was haunted by what-ifs. She was so much more privileged than he, she knew, and yet they seemed to understand each other.

Danil had spoken of *saving* her, because he saw through all the masks she put in place, or tried to.

And yet she did not need saving. Could not accept saving.

This was the circle her mind kept going in—and she could not stop it, because she had no answer. Only the whirl of thoughts and conflicting feelings.

She walked faster along the shore, her boots making squelching sounds in the wet sand. There was a place up here, far away from the castle, where she could hide. Where she could yell and scream and beat her fists against the rock and no one would ever know. No one could see and disapprove. Or send her away.

Where else is there to send you to, Elsebet?

I could save you from that which you do not want.

She squeezed her eyes shut for a few more steps, knowing the way by memory and not needing her sight. She tried to shove it all away, let the wind blow it out of her system. But she felt as she had in that first year here on the island.

Angry, wound tight, ready to blow. Which was why she was heading to her little secret place, which she'd discovered in her first year here. Because as angry as she'd been, then and now, it had never felt right to take her frustrations out on Nielson, Win or Inga. They loved her and cared for her, and she would not take the burden of her feelings out on them.

So she'd walk to the edge of the cove, climb into

the cluster of rocks, and then let it all out any time the frustration overwhelmed her.

Less so lately, but it cropped up every once in a while. A tide that needed to rush in and out before it could settle. The past few days had pushed her to an edge and she needed to let it go.

Lest she explode.

Or make a giant mistake.

She was starting her walk a little late and knew she would not make it to her spot before dark tonight, but it was a clear evening. The sunset would light her way there, the moon would guide her back.

She was practically running now, her breaths coming quickly, and that felt good too. Like she had a million years of unspent energy inside of her that she needed to get out. She made it to the edge of the cove, where rocks and boulders spiraled up and stood shoulder to shoulder. She climbed the familiar footholds that wind and surf had eroded for her. Then she slid down one rock somewhat like a slide and landed on the sand in the middle of a tower of rocks.

No one could see her here, even from the tallest point of the castle. Here in this tiny, *tiny* space she was free to do as she pleased, hidden and muffled by strong, ancient rocks.

So she screamed. She stomped and shouted, and none of it was words or coherent. It was just release. She hit the edge of her hands, where she had the most padding on her palms, against the rock. Not as hard as she could, but hard enough to sting. She even kicked one of the rocks. It was no doubt the most foolish kind of outburst, but she always felt better afterward.

However, today none of the tightness in her chest dissipated, though she kept shouting and flailing about. If anything, she felt angrier. As she stood, practically panting and near tears, she still felt as twisted and confused and full of that boiling energy that threatened to lead her toward mistake.

I could save you from that which you do not want.

But could he save her from knowing she had betrayed everything she had always held dear?

Because she *wanted* to save Mathav, to please her father, to do her duty. She *wanted* to be good so she no longer had to be hidden away. So her father no longer hurt over what he hadn't been able to give his country.

She *wanted* Danil, even though that would ruin all the other things.

So there were no answers. Nothing truly to be saved from. Every choice gave her something she did not want. Something she could not live with.

"That was quite a display."

This time when she screamed, it was out of surprise. She whirled, to find Danil lounging on top of the flattest boulder, looking down at her. He was gilded in moonlight and her heart beat triple time, a strange mix of fear and desire making her feel oddly weightless.

And all those conflicting feelings that had felt barbed and twisted inside of her lifted. Because when he was here, it was clear which want loomed larger than all the others.

Him.

But no… He'd seen her… He'd seen *all that*. Panic shot through her. He wouldn't want anything to do with her now either.

"You shouldn't be out here in the dark alone." His voice had changed after three more days of rest. It sounded less a rasp and more a deep, steady thing. She half believed he could lull the ocean tempests into tranquility with it once his throat was fully healed.

He slid down the rock with the kind of grace she would never have expected of a man of his size or with his injuries.

And then he was in the circle of rocks with her, their bodies creating a kind of cocoon of warmth, while moonlight shone down on them as if to spotlight whatever they chose to do here.

For good or for ill.

She was not sure how long they stood, not speaking, the only sound around them the crashing of the surf very close. The only thing they did was breathe and stare at each other, just out of reach. Both held back by something.

"What bothers you, Elsebet?" he asked into the quiet.

Elsebet. There was something about how he said her name. His accent, perhaps. Or the deep richness of his voice. Something inside of her that was wrong and broken because it felt like a shameful *need* when he spoke her name.

To hear him say it, over and over again. Closer. With his lips on her. With his hands on her.

She swallowed. He had not run away. He had asked her what was wrong. But oh, she could not tell him. He'd likely sail out on the first ship he could.

"I should head back to the castle." She could not trust herself out here in her secret place alone with him. "Nielson will worry."

"No doubt he will. Once he learns you snuck out."

She found she couldn't be surprised that Danil knew. Danil seemed to know and understand everything about her. So she needed to escape.

But neither of them moved.

"Why have you not told them you can speak?" she asked, her voice strained even to her own ears. Because she'd been desperate to know for days but knew the answer would hurt. But here in the rocks and sand she could not seem to do anything but seek out *hurt*.

"I wish to save my voice for when it's important."

She did not miss the meaning. That speaking to *her* specifically was important. Her heart lurched in her chest. That *she* was still important. Even after... screaming and crying?

She knew her *role* was important to her father. She knew Nielson, Win and Inga viewed her as important because of her title.

But no one thought it was important to speak to her. For who she was in this moment. Not a princess.

Just a woman. With feelings so big she needed to let them out.

And he did not express any dismay or disapproval at her ridiculous outburst. He acted as he always did.

"You have always seemed quite sweet and on an

even keel. Is it because when you feel anything else you come here and take it out on the rocks?" He asked it so casually, when it spoke to the deeper parts of herself she always tried to keep hidden.

She looked around at the moonlight space. Too small for the two of them—though any space would feel too small for the two of them right now, she was sure.

She could lie, pretend he hadn't seen what he absolutely had. She could leave. But instead, she told him the truth. Well, part of the truth. "It doesn't seem right or fair to take it out on the rest of them."

For a moment something flickered in his expression. She had seen this before. His reaction to something she said, confusion but something deeper than that. A kind of yearning mixed with distrust.

She would have to know him better to understand this look, and she knew that was not in the cards. Couldn't be.

And still he did not turn her away as though she'd done something wrong.

He cocked his head. "Why not? They *are* your staff, and you *are* their princess, are you not?"

"But they have done nothing wrong. My frustrations are my own. Caused by…"

"Me?" he supplied, but not with any kind of apology. With a silky kind of promise.

"You could say that if you wish to be arrogant, but it isn't so much about you as it is… My feelings are my own, Danil." And he had seen too many of them.

But remained.

He moved closer and she, fool that she was, did not back away. She simply let him take more and more of her space.

Because you wish there to be no space.

He reached out, touched his rough finger to her cheek.

"You saying my name has haunted me for many nights now," he said, his voice getting raspier the more he used it.

As if he felt the same things she did. But was he as conflicted as she was? Did he have a duty awaiting him? He didn't act like it, but she also knew the kind of yearning caused by a duty that chafed and had seen it in his eyes when he'd looked at her art.

Had heard it in his voice when he'd pulled away from her up in her tower. There was *something* in his *I cannot.*

And he was here, touching her face, rather than leaving or telling her she was wrong for having her feelings. If anything, he'd almost validated them.

"Tell me," she said, sounding more fervent than the situation warranted. She reached out and took his hands because she needed answers. She so desperately needed someone to have an answer. "When we were up in my tower, and you said you could not, what did you mean? Exactly."

Danil had known Elsebet had this kind of passion in her—the kind that could make her yell and scream and pound walls. He'd seen glimpses of it—flashes in her eyes, the way she'd kissed him, her own frustration. But he had not realized the depth of it, he supposed. That she worked so hard to suppress it.

He had thought it new. Timid. But no. She kept it on a leash for the sake of those she loved.

It stirred many things inside of him, not the least of which was the heat in his bloodstream, which could not lead them anywhere good. Not here, where no one ever need know…

No one…

But Danil would know. And if he was never to see her again, perhaps he could have lived with that. He could have taken her in his arms, indulged in all that she was and all he could give her.

But he could not live with it and spend the rest of his life watching her be his brother's bride.

And she *would* be his brother's bride. It was Aras's right to have her.

Not Danil's.

"Danil…"

He could not tell her the reason. He could hardly explain she had been promised to his brother. It was clear she had no idea her father had ever made or broken any such promises. She was still locked up here, awaiting her fate. Hiding in these little rocks when she needed a good yell.

It struck him in this moment as decidedly unfair. But then, when did fairness have anything to do with how the world worked? His life had never been *fair*.

Even if he wished the world could give Elsebet better, this was not how anything worked. "You have made it quite clear you have a duty," he said.

She frowned, as if she saw it for the lie it was. But she did not push him. She dropped his hands, turned away. "I need to get back." She began to climb up a rock, as if it was something she did often.

She no doubt did. Isolated herself here where she could scream and yell and curse the world...without hurting the feelings of anyone she cared about.

Had he ever known such selflessness?

This of course did not matter. How it affected him, awed him. Nothing about her mattered because there was only the mission.

He was only The Weapon. Loss would never touch him again, because there was nothing to lose when you were only a tool.

He needed her to *want* to come with him. So he followed behind her, struggling for the words that might get through to her. She was afraid, clearly. Though she was strong and brave in many respects, had built herself into her own woman on this little island with her surrogate family and her art, she was still sheltered. She might *imagine* what was beyond this island, her father's kingdom, but she had no actual knowledge.

Perhaps if he had a few more days, he might find a way to offer that knowledge to her.

Why? So she can go to Gintaras, become Aras's bride, and never see it?

Because Aras would not give her freedom or independence. It was not his way. Everyone in Aras's court had clear roles and strict rules. The women especially. His queen would be the most...

Isolated.

It pained Danil. That word. When Elsebet already felt it so much. When she clearly yearned to see something more.

Something irregular and unknown shifted inside of Danil. He had a debt to pay. He did not go back on his debts, and yet…

He did not wish to see Elsebet trade one prison for another. Even if life was, essentially, its own prison. It was what you did with the duties, responsibilities and debts you owed that mattered—not what those things *were.*

Elsebet would understand that. She had to.

But the sense of unease didn't go away, no matter how hard he tried to push it away. He might have considered that deeper, and it might have fully changed something inside of him, but he saw something…out along the water. Beyond the cove.

A flash of light.

Danil stopped following Elsebet and held himself still. So still he did not dare breathe. It could have been a trick of the eye—that was always possible out in the vast ocean. And it had only been a handful of days. Though the weather had been calm and clear here, that did not mean it had been so between here and Gintaras.

Had a ship truly arrived so quickly?

The light flashed once more. Clear this time. It was the signal.

So it was time to act. There was no more time to think. *To question.*

This was good, he thought to himself. *Insisted* in his own mind. Questions led him nowhere comfortable. Nowhere good.

His ship had come. And here was his moment. It was dark. Nielson would no doubt come looking for Elsebet before long, and when he didn't find either of them, he would sound an alarm.

It wouldn't be enough time, but Danil knew there may be no other moment like this one. She was *right* here. If he followed the narrow beach up and around, the ship wouldn't need to come much closer at all. The danger would be much mitigated if the ship didn't need to try and anchor.

Once he had control of his ship, and Elsebet on it, he could outrun whoever the King of Mathav might send after him. They would still not know *who* had taken her or how. Not right away.

It was now or never, so it had to be now.

Danil caught up with Elsebet, took her by the arm and turned her to face out toward the opening of that cove.

"Do you see that light?" he asked her, pointing. Surprised at how desperate his own voice sounded when he should be calm. Relieved. Ready.

Not panicked.

She looked up at him suspiciously, then out toward the moonlit waves. It took a few humming seconds, but then it flashed. It would not flash again for thirty minutes. This was the signal.

This was his moment. He turned to look at Elsebet and did not understand the way his heart hammered inside him. This was the plan, had always been the plan. He was finally completing his mission. It should feel like relief.

Not like walking along a highwire.

"The time has come, Elsebet. That is my ship. My crew has come to collect me." The weather was perfect. Calm and clear. He did not know who had been assigned the captain's task, but clearly it was someone skillful enough to get here quickly.

He took her hands in his and drew her to him. "Come with me."

She did not pull her hands away, no refusal came from her, and yet… She looked at him, still and silent, for too long. Thinking too much. Thinking would not lead to the decision he needed her to make.

But the words he needed seemed to dry up inside of him. Lies about how he could give her freedom and adventure. When he was only another jailor.

He needed to convince her and quickly. But he could not find the words.

What was *wrong* with him?

Her small hands in his, the moonlight in her hair and her eyes. His little siren, and he was just another cage.

The pressure in his chest built until it wasn't just a lack of words, it was the ability to speak at all.

Perhaps he was having some kind of delayed response to his head injury. An aneurysm.

She tugged her hands, but he could not seem to let himself release her.

"I cannot go with you, Danil," she whispered over the lap of waves that seemed to echo in his ears now.

"You want to," he managed, because he could see she did. She *yearned* to.

"Yes," she agreed, and he thought perhaps he'd won, but she shook her head. "But... I have a duty. To my country, to my kingdom. To my father. Wants have nothing to do with my choices, Danil. They cannot."

Something hot and angry brewed inside of him. That she could so easily refuse him for her duty when he was struggling to do his. That she could look so sad when she was making her own choice. That she could have made this simple thing so damn difficult.

That she, like everyone, would choose something else above him. But why wouldn't she? He was *The Weapon*. Nothing more.

I have a duty, Elsebet had said.

Well, so did he.

He dropped her hands, but before she could turn and make her escape back toward the castle, he swept her up in his arms.

For a moment there was no response as he strode up the rocky shore, Elsebet over his shoulder.

"What are you doing?" she demanded, her voice high and tight, her body rigid with shock.

"My duty," he said grimly. And began to walk toward the sea.

CHAPTER EIGHT

ELSEBET WAS QUITE certain Danil had lost his mind. Maybe he'd never had it in the first place. Maybe he'd lost it during the shipwreck. Maybe he'd always been a raving lunatic but knew how to hide it with helpfulness and seductive smiles.

Either way, he was striding along the lapping waves in the middle of the night, carrying her over his shoulder like she was a sack of flour. Not *into* the ocean exactly, but along the shore. Up toward where the beach got more and more narrow until there was only ocean and cliff wall.

Where that little light had flashed.

He was heading for a ship, *his* ship, while the stars shone above like artwork, and she was bumping against his shoulder like said sack.

It hadn't even occurred to her to fight him, because…what was happening? How did this make any sense when he'd been so terribly injured only a short time ago?

But he had a ship out there. She'd seen the light

herself. He was… He was taking her against her will. Whether she wanted to go or not.

She did *not* want and was a little horrified she had to remind herself of that very fact as he walked purposefully along the beach.

"Danil…" She tried to think rationally over the beating panic. "You must let me go. I don't think you know what you're getting yourself into. Please. My father won't rest. He will come after me. I think you're confused. I think…" Surely he didn't understand her situation. He thought he was saving her, doing something right, perhaps.

He could not be more wrong, of course.

Though he seemed like a man on a mission who understood well enough. And he spoke of duty.

My duty.

His own duty?

And it occurred to her then, oh, far too late, that this was never about *her*—not in the sense she'd fancied it. It wasn't about him understanding her, wanting her, saving her.

This was about the same thing her entire life had been about. Her being the Princess of Mathav. A political pawn. A negotiation term and nothing else.

Those first few days, she'd been suspicious, hadn't she? Then she'd forgotten to be. Because he listened. He smiled. He'd kissed her back like she might be important. Like he might have some way of offering her freedom when she had always known there was no freedom to be had.

He'd looked at her with such *understanding* when

she'd spoken of being a hellion. That little shake of his head, like he couldn't imagine it, had warmed her for days. His kiss. His offer to save her. Speaking of making bread with his grandmother or wondering what might have been different if he'd had a father. Everything he'd done since he'd arrived.

But his *duty* had nothing to do with saving her, nothing to do with *Elsebet*, and everything to do with her being the Princess of Mathav.

She began to struggle then, ashamed it had taken her so long to find the fight within her. She kicked and she punched his back, but it was of course no use. He was so much bigger than her. It didn't even matter that he was injured. He seemed impervious to pain.

"You cannot do this, Danil," she said, trying to sound determined and imperial like her father did when he was angry. It brought tears to her eyes that she only sounded desperate.

"You have left me no choice," he replied grimly, still *walking*. As if this was normal and right. As if she weighed nothing and he hadn't been stitched up and unable to speak only two weeks ago.

My duty.

You have left me no choice.

Choice. He dared speak to *her* of choice. "They will come after you. My father will not rest. This is not the course of action you want to take. I do not know who sent you or what you want…" She wanted to sob then. Because clearly this was about her position, when she'd thought for the first time in her life that something had been about *her*. Else-bet, the woman.

Not the princess-pawn.

He hadn't censured her for her outburst. He'd still wanted her. Or pretended to. It was *all* pretend.

Well, thank goodness she'd chosen her duty. She'd give herself credit for that if nothing else. Maybe she was pathetic, foolish. Maybe she had everything to be embarrassed about, everything to fear as he continued his walk along the sea.

But she hadn't chosen him. She had to hold on to that little sliver of pride. When push came to shove, when wants came against duty, she had chosen Mathav. Her father.

"This will end badly for you, Danil," she said. She did not know how she finally made herself sound strong in the moment, but she did. Even as the pain and betrayal of it washed through her.

He said nothing. He walked on. Splashing in the water as he walked around the cove. She saw no more flashing lights, but he seemed to know exactly where he was going.

"Why? Why are you doing this?" And she knew she did not sound demanding or imperial then. She sounded like a sad child. Perhaps she felt like one. Some part of her had trusted him, even knowing he was a stranger. She had felt something...undefinable. A connection she thought meant something.

She was a fool.

He continued on silently and no amount of fight dislodged his arm banded around her. No amount of struggle stopped his forward movement. He simply *kept going*. Until he was nearly waist-deep in the water. Until she could make out the outline of a small flotation device or raft bobbing ever closer in the bright moonlight.

"I'll… I'll…jump off," she said, trying to dislodge his grip on her. She had to fight. She had to do something aside from feeling so deeply betrayed. She could not let him put her on that ship.

He laughed then, a low rumble that somehow moved through her like heat even when she was so angry. Hurt beyond reason, and still her body reacted to him. How patently unfair.

"You can try, Princess," he said, his voice getting raspier, no doubt the exertion and the speaking working against his injuries.

Good, she thought to herself. He deserved every last one. And more. She would find a way to give him more.

Then and there she decided she would not simply fall apart. She would not let the pain and betrayal fell her.

She had been nothing but a pawn all her life. She had *let* herself be that, but now she was something else. Though she had often felt a prisoner under her father, she had also been in that prison somewhat voluntarily. She had taken it because it was a bit of a punishment she deserved for being so unruly. Because it had been partly her duty. Her legacy. Because if she did her duty, made her father proud, maybe he could look at her and not see her long-lost mother.

Regardless, she had not given in to Danil. Even when she'd desperately wanted to. Which meant she couldn't now. She could not be the person always accepting whatever *men* threw at her.

Now she had to be strong. Now she had to *fight*. When she'd never been taught how. When she'd never allowed herself any true rebellion.

She did not know how to fight yet, not as Danil got her on the raft, not as they were pulled toward a bigger ship. Not as she was lifted from raft to boat against her will.

But she would find out. Danil would not win.

She was the Princess of Mathav, and she would be no one's prisoner ever again.

Danil got Elsebet onto the boat, though it was a struggle. She had fought, and he supposed it was a bit perverse to be proud of her. Glad that she would try to fight rather than cry and take her fate easily.

She was a strong woman. This was good for her future. She would need to be with Aras. That thought felt as cold as the icy water had.

He climbed into the boat himself, trying not to let the physical toll on him show to the men who awaited him. But his injuries from the shipwreck were still not fully healed. He never would have been *breathless* at such exertion before.

He didn't let it show. Not because of Elsebet, though she was clearly angry enough to use it against him, but because he was back on one of his ships. He was captain once more, and the two men who had helped them up were his crew.

Danil breathed a sigh of some relief. This was comfortable, familiar ground. His ship. Him in charge. The dark sea around him and navigating it.

He did not look at Elsebet but kept a good grip on her lest she try to see through her threat to jump off. But looking at her would take away this feeling of sturdy ground. So he nodded at the men. "I was not sure anyone would come," Danil said in his native tongue. He did not think Elsebet spoke it, but he wouldn't put it past her. Still, they'd speak it until he knew for sure. The less she knew the better.

Danil studied the two men who stood before him. Peet had often been on his crew through a variety of missions. He was a good sailor, with good instincts. He could be timid when faced with authority, and had never made the ranks of guard, but Danil always took him on seafaring missions for his proficiency with sailing.

Riks, on the other hand, was a member of King Aras's council. Not much of a sailor in any way, shape or form, so an interesting choice of second man. Especially since he looked a little worse for the wear, as if he'd spent most of the voyage sick.

"The King was quite adamant," Riks said stiffly.

"The Princess is a flight risk as of yet. She will be locked in the captain's quarters at all times, unless I, and I alone, accompany her. Can you handle getting us back to open sea while I get her settled, Peet?"

Peet nodded. "Yes, sir."

Danil kept his grasp on Elsebet's arm and began to

pull her down the deck toward the stairs that would lead them down into the accommodation. She did not resist exactly, nor did she come easily. It indeed needed to be a *pull*.

Her chin was up, her eyes blazed with anger. He had to admit, he'd expected a little bit more weeping and wailing. Actually, he'd expected it to take longer for her to put together that he was not simply taking her because he wanted her, or because she wanted him. He'd thought he might get to Gintaras before she grew cynical enough to see the truth.

But she had put it together quite quickly. It had only taken him calling it a duty for her to realize she remained what she'd always been under her father's thumb. Simply a pawn.

It almost made him sad.

But he pushed that away. Perhaps it was not her fault that she had been put into such a position, but her father should not have broken his promise to Aras.

Danil made it to the captain's quarters. He was pleased to see neither Peet nor Riks had made the mistake of claiming these quarters for themselves. *He* was the captain of the ship. Always.

"This will be your room," he said to the Princess without looking directly at her. "Should you feel sick, there is a bathroom through there. You will sleep here, eat here, but if you behave, I just might let you above board for supervised walks." He knew it was too harsh. Honey attracted better than vinegar and all that.

But something he did not recognize held him in its

grip and the only way he could see his way through it was to be cruel.

"So this is to be my dungeon?" she said, chin up and eyes hard. Nothing siren about them now. Just cold.

He refused to let the guilt take a hold. He looked around the room. The nice bed. The separate bathroom with a door. It smelled nice and clean. He sneered at her, compelled by all this anger inside of him. "If you think you can call this a dungeon, *Your Highness*, you have clearly never been in one."

"And you have?"

He said nothing to this question, meant to be impertinent when it was anything but. He thought his silence was terrifying enough, but he did not understand the way her expression changed. From fury and defiance to something sad. "Why would you have been in a dungeon, Danil?" she asked softly. Gently. Almost as if she'd reach out and touch his chest like she had in her art gallery.

Almost like she cared.

But her expression changed as she said his name. "Danil," she repeated. Then she laughed. Bitterly. "Is that even your name?"

"It is. I have no need to hide who I am, Princess. Not behind my art or in secret-rock hiding places."

Her eyes narrowed. Fury practically leaped from her, and again he felt that backward pride that she would have such fire in her.

"No one from nowhere?" she said, all scathing bitterness.

"I am Danil Laurentius, also known as *The*

Weapon. Head of the Gintaras King's Guard and Navy. Your father promised you to our king, and so you will be delivered to him."

"If my father promised me to your king, I would be with him. This surely would not need to be so cloak-and-dagger."

"Your father broke his promise. And he should be grateful that my brother's only revenge is to take you by force. He could do worse."

Elsebet was silent for a few humming moments. Danil needed to take his leave, he knew he did. Lock her in here and take over as captain. Breathe the sea air and find his footing once more.

But he did not move.

"You'll deliver me to your king, and then what?" Elsebet asked, very, *very* quietly.

And when he spoke, his own voice sounded strangely quiet, oddly strangled. Not the rasp of his injuries, but something else. Something he could not acknowledge. "You shall be his bride. The Queen of Gintaras."

"Is that what you want, Danil?"

He looked at her then, because *want*? He wanted to laugh in her face, but he only spoke the truth. "Have you learned nothing, Elsebet? Our wants do not matter. There is only duty. And I am better at doing mine than you or your father are at doing yours." He wrenched open the door. "You will be locked in. There is an intercom should you need anything."

He did not slam the door behind him, though he wanted to. He simply pulled it closed, ensured it was locked, then strode away. Up to the captain's seat. Where he would guide his ship back to Gintaras.

Because he was *The Weapon*, and that was his mission, and any feelings swirling inside of him like their own dark tempest did not matter.

Ever.

CHAPTER NINE

SINCE SHE WAS ALONE, and it seemed unlikely anyone would return right away, Elsebet let herself cry. She did not *only* cry. She also planned. But the tears streamed down her cheeks as she planned.

Her heart felt bruised. And she wanted only anger and hatred, but… Oh, she knew better than to think him not answering her question about what he wanted might *mean* something. She would be a fool to believe *he* had also felt the connection between them that she had, or kissed her and spoken of saving her because he *wanted* to.

But her heart *had* nursed that notion, and apparently her heart was a fool.

What did it matter anyway? Regardless of what he wanted, he was taking her to his country, his king. Giving her away. Choosing his *duty*, just as she'd chosen hers.

But something eased inside of her. That this might be duty over want. Believing, no matter how her brain told her not to, that he didn't *want* to hand her over to his king. Maybe she hadn't been so *totally* fooled.

Maybe there was some…side of him that felt some of the things she felt. She had seen yearning in his eyes. She had *felt* his response to her when she touched him, kissed him.

Surely such things couldn't be faked…could they?

She didn't know. So she cried nearly silently and she searched the entire room. She didn't know exactly what she was looking for. A weapon? A way out? A telephone? *Something* that might give her a chance.

But the room was essentially empty aside from bedding and toiletries. There was a tiny circular window, but it was dark outside, so there was nothing to see.

There was a little desk connected to the wall and she looked through its contents, finding a few pens and pencils. She looked at the door.

When she'd been a little girl in the palace, she had often tried to learn how to pick locks. She'd never gotten very far. A chaperone always showed up before she could accomplish anything, and the palace locks were much different than anything on this ship.

But what did it lose to try? She had literally *nothing* to lose at this point.

So she knelt at the door with the pens and pencils gripped in her hand, studying the lock. It did not look as though it locked from the outside, but when she tried to turn the knob it didn't budge. So there had to be some sort of mechanism.

Maybe it was a pointless endeavor, but it gave her something to focus on. She took apart one pen, used the bits and pieces to poke at the lock.

She could not give up. She had to find a way out. *What then? You're on a ship.*

She could jump overboard, of course, but they'd likely sailed far away enough from shore that a swim home wouldn't be possible.

Would she rather die than be taken to a king, drown in the vast ocean?

She knew nothing about this king. Was it really so different than what her father had planned for her? Wasn't he also planning on delivering her to a stranger?

Except she liked to think her father would have given her information. Time to come to grips with the upcoming change in her life. Meet the man a few times, maybe even ask her opinion.

When has your father ever listened to your opinion? She pressed her forehead to the door, trying to stem the tide of tears. It didn't matter what her father would have done.

Danil was giving her *nothing*.

Because this was his duty.

Why can you not think of him as the villain in this story when it is nothing but clear?

She focused anew at poking the bits of pen and pencil into the lock mechanism wherever she could manage. Nothing changed. Nothing budged, but she thought she heard a faint *click*. Maybe she'd—

The door swung open and she stumbled back, fell on her bottom.

Danil stood there in the space he'd opened. He

frowned down at her. "You should have rested," he said, looking down at her with some hint of—

No, she had to stop letting her heart think he might be looking at her in any specific way. She was his prisoner and he was her kidnapper. There were no feelings here.

If only.

"How do you know I did not?" she returned, trying to make her position on the floor look purposeful. She shook her hair back and looked around imperially. "Is there some sort of surveillance watching my every move in here?"

"There are bags under your eyes, Princess. And the fact you're still in wet clothes." He held out his hand, as if she should take it so he could help her to her feet. "You need to take those damp, dirty skirts off."

She did not take his hand, and she considered remaining seated on the floor. She was a prisoner— why not lounge on the hard floor as part of the whole thing? But he was so *tall*, so intimidating as he loomed above her. She couldn't feel on *even* ground, but she had to claim some kind of power.

She got to her feet herself. Her skirts *were* wet, and she was uncomfortable, but it matched her gloomy mood. "And wear what? You did not leave me any dry clothes."

He moved toward the little built-in closet that she'd already snooped through but had only found empty. He opened the door, then stopped. He frowned a little, as if he had not expected to find it empty. But the frown was quickly replaced by something far more stoic. He closed the door, turned to face her. "Take them off and get under the covers," he said pointing to the bed.

Elsebet looked down at her skirts, then at the bed, then at the way he stood there, arms folded like he was just going to…watch.

Which sent a wave of heat through her. The idea of him watching her take off her clothes. Even if she left her undergarments on, he'd see more of her than he had before. She'd felt his hands on her, but only through fabric.

The idea of his bare hands on her bare skin…

You are fantasizing about the man who just kidnapped you against your will.

And yet she couldn't break his gaze, couldn't ice away the heat inside of her. Whatever this was, she did not seem to have any control over what it did to her body. And with her body *reacting*, her brain seemed to weaken. She couldn't hold on to those *rational* thoughts.

She was lost in the dark brown of his eyes, the memory of his mouth on hers. The size and heat of him when she pressed herself to him. The way he'd looked at her art, his heart thumping under her hand as he'd offered to save her.

A lie.

She struggled to care.

"You want me to take off my clothes?" she said, breathless.

He stood so still she could have mistaken him for a statue, if not for the heat in his eyes. "My king would not be very happy with me if I brought him a flu-ridden bride. You should get dry and warm."

My king. Bride. He was taking her to a stranger. When he'd held her and kissed her and walked with her. When he'd looked at her art with yearning and not been offended by her outburst in her hideout.

It twisted in her, dark and angry, but she was sad and hurt too. And for the first time in her life, she wanted to take her hurt out on somebody. On him. She *wanted* him to hurt the way she did. Feel as conflicted as she had from the moment she'd laid eyes on him.

She could not hurt him physically. Her only hope was that…he *did* yearn for her. After all, his voice sounded rough. Maybe it was his injuries. Who could say, but she thought she saw anguish in his gaze. She knew she *wanted* to see some there. And maybe it was a figment of her imagination that he might be struggling with the same thing she was.

Desire. Even with all this complication, all this betrayal. If he really *did* want her, if that anguish was real…couldn't she torture *him* with it? Couldn't she use it, the way he'd used hers to get her here?

My king, he'd said, as if she was only a prize to be doled out. Well, maybe that was all she would ever be. But if she was a prize for the King to win, that meant Danil was the loser. Maybe she could make him *feel* it.

He began to turn his back to her, some nod to privacy, perhaps? But the anger in her boiled and she spoke, hoping to keep his attention.

"Will your king be happy with me?" she asked,

innocently enough. But she reached back and pulled down the zipper of her dress. She held his gaze the entire time. "Do you think he'll find me attractive? Want to kiss me? Touch me?" Her voice faltered at *touch*, because she pictured Danil being the one to do these things.

But she did not stop.

"I have not been truly *touched*, as I'm sure you're aware if you're doing this for your king. Maybe everyone in the world is aware." A bitter thought for a bitter moment.

She had been told over and over again, in such vague terms it had taken her a long, long time to understand, that her virginity would be seen as an asset. If Danil was taking her to his king, Danil must know this about her.

Would it be appealing to *him*? It had certainly been talked about as if it was the be-all and end-all in royal weddings. No matter what she'd heard, she'd never been able to understand *why* her virginity mattered. Only that it *did,* to some.

The men who would want her, anyway.

She surveyed Danil now as she let the dress shimmy off her, until she was standing in her undershirt that skimmed her upper thighs, and the thick stockings that might have kept her warm if they weren't damp from the ocean.

Because *he* had dragged her through it. *He* had taken her against her will. She wished this would cool any of the things happening in her body, but no. Her body was its own riot of reaction. That throbbing, that wanting. Wrong and traitorous, yes, but it kept her going. Because if Danil was having these same reactions inside of him, if he wanted her and took her…

He would not be able to deliver her to his king. Not without something coming back on him. This would be revenge.

And adventure.

Because, though it shamed her to admit, it was nothing but true. Even when she saw him as the very devil, her body still reacted to him in such a way she did not think it would be a *physical* hardship, while it would certainly be an emotional one.

She had two choices. She could either go to his king untouched, allowing Danil to do his duty while she had *nothing* for herself, or she could have this thing she wanted, even if she shouldn't, and then be delivered to this king all the same.

Well, why not take what she wanted in this moment? Why not give herself *something* on the way to being yet another man's pawn?

She walked over to the bed, which put her closer to him. He stood *very* still. So still she knew it was a reaction. No one was ever that still when *nothing* was going on inside them.

Besides, his eyes never left her body.

She sat down, rolled the wet stockings off her legs, watching him through her eyelashes. His gaze followed the move of each stocking, roamed the exposed leg. Yes, he wanted her. And if she gave herself to him, she would have something she wanted *and* revenge.

Though her arms shook—a mix of fear and excitement—she lifted her shirt over her head and let it fall to the ground with her damp stockings. She was in nothing but her underwear, sitting on the edge of the bed. He had moved in that short time, but only a few inches.

Closer.

She couldn't help but think he wasn't aware that he'd done that, when it seemed like Danil *always* knew what he was doing.

But he wanted her. She could see the evidence of his own arousal, jutting against the fabric of his pants. His expression *had* changed. Gone fierce. On her. As if he was cataloging every inch of exposed skin.

He wanted to touch her. She had no doubts in this moment, hot and potent. Maybe she had no knowledge of men and women, of the world outside her little island and a palace in Mathav. But she knew Danil. And she could seduce him. She could ruin *his* plans.

The knowledge speared through her like power, twisting with the desire of her body.

She would find some of her own pleasure, because no matter how this had all gone disastrously wrong, no matter how she could never forgive him for what he'd done to her, she knew he would bring her pleasure.

And that was something no one would ever be able to take away from her. Not her father, not his king. It would be hers and hers alone.

Finally.

She stood and moved toward him, gratified when

he moved, like he was about to take a step back and only at the last moment stopped himself. Wants fighting with duties. Pride fighting with desperation.

She felt her own war over both those things, but if she had to be kidnapped and taken away to some unknown king, and not even for her father and her duty, why shouldn't she have some pleasure before her life was over?

This wouldn't be for Danil. It wouldn't be for any dreams that he might have a change of heart if she shared her body with him. This was just for experience. For curiosity. For, at least this once, getting something *she* wanted. So she crossed to him.

"Your clothes are damp still, Danil. Perhaps *you* should take them off as well. And join me under the covers."

She reached out with the idea to help him, or run her hands over his chest, *something* to close this distance between them, but he took her by the wrists before she could. For a moment, she thought it was to stop her, push her away. But instead he drew her closer, tilting his head down.

She raised her mouth, certain his would touch hers. Certain he would kiss her like he had at the beach, dark and desperate. And oh, how she *yearned* for that. For the way sensation could obliterate all rational thought.

But he didn't kiss her. He lowered his mouth beyond her lips and to her ear. He spoke, the vibration of his voice against her ear making her shudder with need. Even as his words landed like blows.

"I see what you're planning, Princess, and while it's quite a cunning choice to try to rid yourself of your innocence, it would only end in your death." He dropped her hands, glared down at her. "So I would not recommend it."

Elsebet's eyes widened. Her hand came up before Danil had even gotten the rest of the words out, but she was clearly not used to striking people, because it was easy enough to catch her by the wrist and stop her palm from making contact with his cheek.

Though a blow might have done him some good. Heaven knew he deserved it.

He'd stopped her from slapping him because he was afraid if he let her make contact, it would snap this little bit of control he'd managed to maintain.

When control had never, ever been the issue. Control was who he was.

But she tested *everything*.

He wanted her. A want so all-encompassing he was sure he'd never survive it. Because he'd never wanted for anything this much. He was a practical man. He had always known wants were not for him. Even when his life had been small and full of love, they had been poor. In need.

He'd known.

He was *The Weapon*, even before that had been a nickname. He was not Danil Laurentius. He was a tool for everyone else. His mother's husband. His brother. It did not matter. He'd been made to be a tool.

This had always been a comfort to him as Aras's

right hand. Always. But tonight it felt like a prison. With memories of cozy dinners with Elsebet and her little faux family. He hadn't been a tool or weapon among them. Just family. Just like the one he'd had as a boy.

And now he was a man with Elsebet nearly naked before him. Perfect in every way. And he knew she desired him. This was not *all* put-upon. But she wanted to give herself to him in this moment so his brother would not want her, or so he would be punished, or *something*. She wanted to share herself with him to *hurt* his plans.

"It would end in my death?" she replied, trying to laugh, but it just came out a kind of breathless sound that drew his gaze to her mouth. It mattered not that it had been nearly two weeks since he'd done it, he could relive every second of their kiss on the beach. Her taste, her warmth.

Sunlight in a dark storm, and oh, how this felt like a storm.

She is not yours. She is Aras's.

"My king was promised a virginal princess. He would not take kindly to finding you were not the innocent he wanted." For the purposes of heirs. For the purpose of having more people under his thumb.

Danil tried to forget these traitorous thoughts. She was nothing but a siren, putting lies into his brain. He served his brother, because his brother was king, and as such held all the power. All the wants.

This was right, or at the very least, the way of things.

And still he did not drop the wrist he held, did not

leave, did not look away from the sweet swell of her breasts, rising and falling in heavy breaths.

But he was not kind. "If this is so offensive to you, I'm afraid you'll have to take that up with your father. Once you are able, of course."

"Does it matter?" she asked, and her eyes were full of so many emotions that twisted his heart, that reminded him of places he'd been. At the mercy of his mother's husband. An angry king—his biological father. Then dungeons. So tired of being twisted around by everyone else's plans that he didn't think anything he'd ever say or do or want would matter.

To anyone.

It matters to her.

He looked at her in the eyes, those dark, midnight blue eyes. The first time he'd seen her he thought they promised storms, and he had been right. She was nothing but a storm inside of him, no matter how small and placid she seemed.

Her breath came in pants, and he did not feel as though he had *any* power. Because her lips were pink and glossy. Her skin, as creamy as any delectable dessert. How he wanted to taste her. Everywhere.

Would she taste of the sea in every swell, every dip, in the sweetest places of her? The pain became so sharp he wondered if he'd survive it.

"You want me," she whispered.

There was no point lying. This was the simplest truth and she knew. It was no question. It required no affirmation, but it was drawn out of him all the same. "Yes."

He would have to face his brother. He would have to face her as his *queen*. Already it seemed torture, and all he'd done was kiss her. Once.

But he could not deny that he wanted her. With every fiber of his being. He was so hard he ached. So drunk on the scent of her, the blue of her eyes and the yearning in them. He could not seem to uncurl his hand from her wrist. Soft like velvet, small and in need of protection.

She is not yours to protect.

But those siren eyes told another story.

"Danil. Your king would never have to know it was you."

His breathing became labored then, because the quiet whisper of that possibility was insidious. Aras would know.

How?

"Have you ever been allowed anything you wanted, Danil?" she asked him then, almost desperate. Her hand curled into a fist, but still she did not wrench it away. Still her eyes were wet. Still…she seemed to understand, even after he'd betrayed her.

Had he ever had anything he wanted? In his whole life? His ships, the comradery from his army of guards and sailors, but all these things had to be kept at a careful distance lest Aras see they meant too much and take them away.

To make you a better weapon…

"We recognize each other, because we are the same inside," Elsebet said, like she was so sure. Like she knew everything and he knew nothing. "Yearning for something. For freedom. You cannot offer me any, but you can give me this. Give me this."

She reached out and took his hand. He could not stop her. He could not seem to get his muscles to work, when he was the strongest man he knew. She pulled his arm and his hand went to her. She pressed his palm to her chest.

"Touch me."

It did not feel like a ploy, like an attempt to get out of having to marry Aras or some twisted desire to see him punished.

Her demand felt only like truth.

CHAPTER TEN

ELSEBET'S HEARTBEAT ECHOED in her ears like gunfire. His hand was hot, pressed to her skin. He had wars in his eyes, and she wanted to give him peace.

Even if he'd kidnapped her. Even if he'd hurt her. She saw herself in his inner conflict.

Wanting to do your duty.

And wanting what you *actually* wanted, no matter how opposing those two things were.

He did not pull his hand away. He spread his fingers wide, the rough skin of his fingers sending a cascade of sensation over her chest. Warmth spread after, lower.

His other hand still held her wrist, as if he was afraid she would turn away, when she was the one initiating this. Insisting on this. She'd forgotten all about punishing him, about hating him.

Her heart was too soft, no doubt, but she only wanted what they could make each other feel. If their duty lay on the other side, so be it, but first they had an entire ocean journey.

And she wanted him. Not punishment, not freedom.

Him.

Slowly, impossibly slowly, he tilted his head down closer and closer, until she could count each individual whisker. The stitches Nielson had put in there two weeks ago now. Fading bruises and healing scrapes.

He had risked his life to kidnap her for his king. She should hate him for this alone.

And yet she could not find any hate within her in this moment.

His nose practically touched hers, his eyes dark and ablaze. Their breath mingled, their breathing moved in time. Loud against the quiet of the room. They watched each other, as if they were still waiting for some reason to stop. Some reason to save themselves from this temptation, this want.

Every moment of her life that came before had been a series of not choosing her wants. Even out on that beach tonight, she had chosen duty. But duty had been taken away from her. So she let it go. She reached up on her toes and pressed her mouth to his, much as she had back on the beach that night.

There was a moment of tenderness. Just sweetness and warmth as he kissed her back with a kind of gentle care that made her eyes prickle with tears. And with that, her anger at him fully melted away until nothing was left.

Maybe she should not be so soft, but she could not help but think they were both prisoners in this strange life.

So why not take a moment to enjoy a bright spot?

His lips trailed down her neck. His mouth hot, stirring fires of need inside of her she did not know how to survive. He slid the straps of her bra off her shoulders, pressing kisses there as his hands slid over her rib cage, then tugged the bra down.

Cool air teased her, but only for a few seconds before it was replaced by his mouth, his open kisses, his tongue. The sensation of his mouth on her breast arrowed through her, a lightning strike. Electric and thrilling.

And he stayed there, right there, feasting on her as she grew more and more incoherent, the only thought in her head *more*.

She didn't recognize the noises that came out of her mouth, didn't know what else to do but writhe and gasp under his attention. She wanted more, but she wanted this. She wanted, wanted, wanted.

His hands, so large, so rough, touched every part of her, until it felt as though he possessed her. Every inch of her was his. His, his, his.

He slid the underwear off her hips, and still he did not touch her where she throbbed. "Danil."

But he silenced her with his mouth on hers once more. A kiss as wild as any ocean storm. Him holding her so close she could feel the hard length of him pressed to her. His hands tangled into her hair, possessive and needy.

She would give him everything he needed if only he'd help her find that which her body pounded for.

"Please," she murmured against his mouth when she thought her legs might give out. When she thought she might simply swoon if she did not get *more*.

He pulled his mouth away, even drew her away by her shoulders, cold air sliding between them. She was naked. He was fully dressed. Elsebet blinked. She had never been fully drunk before, maybe a little tipsy on New Year champagne, but not *drunk*.

This felt like that must. Not just a little giggly and out of sorts, but fully unbalanced. And wonderful, in the moment. She tried to reach for him, to find anchor in him, to touch him in *any* of the ways he'd touched her.

But he stopped her, shook his head. "Sit."

Her breath caught at the command, at the look in his eyes. She did not think twice. She sat.

He crouched before her, spreading her legs wide. There was some dim thought to modesty, but it never fully formed. He looked at her with such hunger, and she was nothing but a mass of hypersensitized cells that clamored for the release she had only read about or found for herself.

His finger traced up her inner thigh, and she watched its journey in utter fascination. The long, rough, blunt shape of his finger against the soft, pale skin of her thigh. Then tracing the seam of her, through the triangle of curls. His finger, touching the most intimate part of her.

She watched, fascinated. She watched, as a feeling so complex and threaded together with sensation swept through her. She did not have the words to express what was happening.

His finger tracing patterns, finding places that made her gasp, sigh, moan. She wanted to close her eyes, drop her head back, get lost, but as if sensing this, he looked up at her in that instant.

Their eyes locked, clashed, and she could not look away. She walked some highwire of this needy, sensual dance. She could not break his heavy gaze. Until he lowered his head as if...

And then there was no doubt. His tongue touched her, licked deep into her like she was a delectable treat. Devouring her. Chasing ribbons of feelings and desires and needs. Until she was shaking, begging, pulsing apart like something had *exploded* within her.

But he didn't stop. He nibbled his way out and then back in. His dark hair between her legs, his clever mouth, the sensations warring inside of her. Like an epic battle and she did not know who or what would come out on top, only that wreckage would be left behind and that would be all right.

More than.

There was no way of knowing. What it felt like to have another person touch you as reverently as a beautiful piece of sea glass. The way a mouth could send her flying to places she'd never been. Waves of feeling, of pleasure. A storm, wild and beautiful. The kind she'd always dreamed of sailing into.

They had both chosen their duty, but they had not known. If they had known *this*, surely they would have chosen each other.

She was shattered, sated. Made new by him. She wanted to reach for him, but he...

He stood. Wound so tight, holding himself back. All for his duty. And because in this moment more than any of the others she understood how much this sacrifice meant to him, even if she didn't know why, she did not press.

"This must be enough," he ground out. Sounding as in pain as he had when he'd been washed ashore, broken and bloody.

"No. It is not enough."

"Elsebet, we cannot."

Cannot. So many cannots between them. But his anguish was too much for her. She understood. He could do this act because it was not irrevocable. In some archaic world, he had not taken her virginity here. She could still be "pure" for this king.

Maybe it should have hurt more than it did. But she understood the complicated, thorny tentacles of duty too well. He'd given her all he could.

So she must give him all she could. She pushed herself up, then slid off the bed and kneeled for him, though he made a move to stop her. But she would not let him.

"Elsebet," he ground out. Not refusal. Not even warning. She thought it was a plea—only even in the depths of his soul she did not think he knew what he asked for.

So she would show him.

"I have read about this," she told him. And truth be told, in books it had seemed rather strange, but faced with the powerful length of him, the way he had made feelings and sensation cascade throughout her body again and again, she wanted to give him the same.

She wanted to give him everything.

* * *

Danil knew he should stop this. It was already too far. Even if he did not tell Aras what had happened here, Danil would spend the rest of his life with Elsebet's taste on his tongue.

Knowing she was his brother's.

But she pulled the zipper down on his pants, freed him with her delicate hands. Soft and warm as she stroked him with a noise of appreciation.

There was no power in the world that could stop this. If there was, he did not have access to it. He wanted her too much, and if he could not have all… couldn't he have some?

She leaned forward, touched her tongue to him. So innocent, so eager. His perfect princess.

He forgot who he was. No longer *The Weapon*. Not bastard son of the old king. No, he was simply Danil.

And his beautiful Elsebet, with her small hands and clever mouth. Those beautiful eyes looking right up at him as she took him deep.

Her blond hair spread out over her shoulders, the sweet way she used her tongue, and the avid exploration as if every move was reverent. He had already been too close to the pounding release just from touching her, kissing her, tasting her.

And now she pushed him over that last edge so quickly, with a climax so powerful, he felt, for the first time in his entire life, weak-kneed and uncertain. More so than when he'd woken up bloody and bruised on a very cold beach.

But Elsebet only smiled up at him as she got to her

feet. "Thank you," she said, putting her palm to his chest as she had so many times now. As if she liked to feel the *thud* of his heart beating.

When he'd forgotten he had one there in the first place. Purposefully. He knew what he'd done was wrong, but in this moment, his blood still pounding loudly in his ears, he could only cover her hand with his and watch as her smile grew wider. Beaming at him.

But a little shiver ran through her—not excitement, but the cool air taking the heat out of her cheeks. "You're cold," he murmured, nudging her back onto the bed and pulling the covers around her. He zipped up his pants, then picked up her discarded clothes and carefully laid them out across the desk and chair so they would dry by morning.

Morning. He would still not face Aras yet. There would be days more at sea. But that would not change the ending.

"Come. Sit," Elsebet ordered him. He should not, this he knew. Staying solved nothing.

Unfortunately at this juncture, neither did leaving. So he returned to the bed and took a seat next to her.

"What troubles you?" she asked, reaching out and brushing her fingers over his now disheveled hair. He would have to fix that before he returned to the captain's chair.

Which he should do. But he sat. *What troubles you?*

It was no use to tell her. This whole interlude was pointless. He should leave. But her hand slid over his shoulders, wrapping him in a hug that was somehow casual and intimate and all-encompassing at once.

He dared not look into her siren eyes or he would be lost once more. So he stared at the empty built-ins where his clothes should have been. But they had been cleaned out.

Because they'd all thought him dead, no doubt. Someone had decided he no longer owned his fleet. No longer existed. And all he was should be erased.

Had anyone mourned?

It should not matter. It *did not* matter. He was *The* Weapon. Or had been until this moment, when he'd betrayed everything. And still he did not push Elsebet's arms off him, or move away from her. He sat. He stared. He spoke.

"I have betrayed the man I owe my life to."

"Why do you owe him your life?"

"He saved mine. I would be dead, many years ago, if he had not interceded."

Elsebet grew very quiet for a time. But her arms stayed around him. The soft warmth of everything she was. Sweet and kind, with a head full of dreams she had been too practical to believe in. When someone like her should have all the dreams reality allowed.

"So you've spent the years since…working for him? As payment?"

It was not so simple as that, but he did not know how to explain to her the complexities in their situation. That his mission was to turn her over not just to his king, but to his *brother*.

"I think… I understand this. It is like me going to my secret place to scream and yell. Knowing Nielson, Win and Inga did so much *for* me, I did not wish to burden them with my own feelings."

"I am not sure how this is the same."

"Not life and death, I grant you. But service born of gratitude."

"I suppose."

"This is different, though, Danil. It is about more than sparing your king's feelings. It is about the way I am being treated like I am property. My father is included in this. We can dress it up in duty, but at the end of the day, I cannot be simply *happy* to do my duty when it is against the things I want."

"I have no wants, Elsebet. It is not for me."

She shook her head. "You *do*. And you have a right to those. You aren't property any more than I am. We are *people*. Not inanimate objects with no feelings or needs of our own. And your king should not feel betrayed that he did not get the pretty little piece of property he wanted when there are plenty more out there."

He looked at her then. So beautiful and fierce. That kindness inside of her, those feelings did not make her weaker somehow. She seemed…strong. Stronger than any screaming threats he'd seen in his day.

He agreed that *she* should not be treated in such a way, but him? "I am *The Weapon*."

Her mouth turned downward in disapproval. "That is a foolish notion. You are a man." She placed her hand over his heart, where it beat and he wished it did not. He had so many wishes, and none of them mattered.

"I have never been one. Not until you came along. You have changed me, Elsebet, but I could not possibly be…" What did he wish for? A life where he could be hers? Where he could live as a humble sailor and soldier, with a wife to come home to.

When she was a *princess*. Who would marry a king or prince no matter if he delivered her to Aras or her family back on the island.

He had no rights to her, no matter what he wished. But…could he really just deliver her, against her will, to Aras now? Beyond what they had just shared of each other, he was not sure he could hand her over to his brother knowing how cruel and harsh Aras could be when angry.

"What is it you want, Elsebet?" he asked, not sure he'd ever be able to give it to her. But he could try. "To return to the island? Your father?"

She stared at him quietly, searching his face for something. He did not think she found it. "You would get in trouble, would you not?"

He thought of Aras. His brother. Danil had never once considered returning as a failure. Never wondered what might happen, because he didn't tolerate the possibility.

Now, for the first time, he considered.

Would his brother be forgiving? He had been the one to save Danil. The only one who'd ever seen him as anything *useful*. Not because of the blood that ran in his veins, but because of what he could *do*.

And still… Danil had seen Aras do many terrible things to those who failed him. Sometimes, his own blood relations. Their father included.

Danil had no fond feelings for the sadistic, former king, but he thought on it now. Would *he* have sentenced the man, his own father, to death if *he* were in charge?

"Danil?"

He shook his head. Surely his brother would not put him to death? Surely…

"I do not wish to see you in trouble," she said earnestly. "I do not wish to worry that you are harmed because of *me*."

"Whatever failures there are, they are mine."

She rolled her eyes at him. It should be incredibly insulting. She shook her head and gestured around the room. "You did not break any promises here. I am no expert on the technicalities, but I'm sure I will appear every bit the virgin. If it is what you wish, I will go to your king. Willingly."

He frowned at her, beyond confused. She had just said she didn't want to be property. She had been so mad he'd taken her, and now… Now she'd given herself to him, in a way. And she was willing to give herself to Aras? "Why? Why would you do such a thing?"

Her eyes tracked over his face, and he *felt* the warmth of her feelings. He did not understand how.

But he could *feel* her care. "Because it would ease your pain," she said softly. Then she leaned forward and pressed a soft kiss to his brow. Like she was taking care of him once more.

"You will take me to your king. He will know nothing that happened here, but I will endeavor to talk him out of the marriage. Surely I can appeal to his heart."

Heart? Did Aras have one? Danil had always thought he meant *something* to his brother. Or why would he have been saved?

But after watching Elsebet and her staff… He did not think his brother had ever cared for him the way Elsebet's little family cared about each other. He did not think he himself had cared for Aras in such a way. Their relationship was duty. Missions to accomplish. Danil had left the idea of family behind when his grandparents had died and his mother had married a despicable man.

"This is what we'll do," Elsebet said, Princess to the last, as though she got to decide. Perhaps he should let her—it was likely she'd never really decided anything in her life. And if anyone could get through Aras, it would be Elsebet.

But he feared she would not. And she would be married to him and Queen of Gintaras before she even had a chance to argue.

He could not let her sacrifice herself so he wouldn't get into trouble. He would have to do something else.

But he didn't have to tell her that. So he nodded,

and encouraged her to get some rest before he left and headed back to the captain's seat.

He would guide the ship back to Gintaras.

And he would take on his brother himself.

CHAPTER ELEVEN

ELSEBET SLEPT LIKE the dead. Exhausted, sated and determined—all conditions making it possible for her to sleep for hours and hours. When she woke, she was groggy and starving.

She stretched and looked around the room. There was nothing to eat here, but she could get dressed and see if Danil had kept her locked in here or not. Her clothes were draped over the chair and table.

Danil had carefully laid them out to dry last night. She wondered why the memory of such a simple act spread through her like warmth, like care. Particularly when the man had *kidnapped* her last night. And yet no amount of reminding herself of this fact changed how she felt.

Particularly knowing he felt he owed his king his life, but still…cared enough for her to risk something. It left a fluttering in her chest that threatened all sane, rational thinking.

She blew out a breath while considering what to do, but really there was nothing else to do but attempt to find food.

But before she could throw off the covers, the door eased open. Slowly at first, then Danil saw that she was awake and entered quickly.

He closed the door behind him. "You must get dressed," he said, nodding toward the clothes on the chair and desk.

She considered this. After last night, she thought she might be able to tempt him again. But where would that lead? His guilt and self-condemnation. Even if she got something pleasurable out of it, it would only be momentary.

That had been enough last night, but today she felt differently. Getting something for herself was selfish, even if she'd wanted him to have his wants too. Because wants were not so easy, this she knew. She had been burdened by duty too.

He was risking something with her. A risk far larger than her own. Because whether she married his king, or the man her father chose, her future was the same. A political affiliation with a stranger, no love.

However, Danil risked punishment, perhaps even his life. And she… Oh, she had been so angry at him last night and it had melted away, like she was so simple that a soft touch and a kiss would change everything she knew to be true.

But it had. What he risked changed the tenor of everything. He was as conflicted as she. How could she hold him at fault for that? How could she be angry when he had his own debts and duties?

Ones that, if he did not fulfill, could claim his life. And she could not bear the thought of his life being taken away. So she would do whatever she could to ensure Danil did his duty, even if it went against hers.

Was this love? In some ways, she thought it was. Because she understood the things inside of him that felt like the things inside of her. But she also understood there were other things locked in Danil's mind and heart that she did not know or understand.

Could you love a person knowing they had secrets and mysteries? A whole past that she did not know, and might not ever?

Could she marry someone else thinking she might be in love with Danil?

If it saved him, the answer was yes. She would sacrifice for him, because… He had given her something no one else had. Even during a kidnap.

She slid out of bed but brought the blanket with her. Not so much out of modesty, but because she did not wish to tempt him in this moment. She wished to give him everything he needed.

She got dressed under the blanket, focusing on the clothes and not whether he watched her or not. Once she was finished, he nodded toward the door.

"Come," he said stiffly.

So she did. She followed him out the door, down the narrow corridor that gave the impression of three other rooms below deck. Then they went up the stairs and onto the deck. Last night had been dark and she'd been angry, so she had no idea what to expect, but it wasn't blinding brightness. She was surrounded by blues that melded together in waves that made her dizzy.

The boat itself wasn't *exceptionally* large, though it was a little bigger than the small royal cruiser that had taken her from Mathav to her island when she'd been thirteen.

Danil took her by the arm and led her forward. Right toward the edge of the ship where, if she looked over the railing, she could see the ship cruising through the ocean.

Nothing but ocean. Blue everywhere. Everywhere she looked. Water and sky. *"Oh."* It was…more amazing than she could have imagined. She had lived with the ocean every day of her life, but almost always from land. Not from the center of it. Not when there was nothing for the eye to see but water and sky. "Oh, Danil." She wanted to lean into him, but he kept inches between them, even with his arm still on her arm as if steadying her.

"The one behind us works for my brother," he said, speaking of the other man out on the deck. "I do not trust him."

Elsebet looked over at the man. He was watching them rather intently from the other side of the ship, but too far away to hear them speaking. She was more concerned with how Danil's brother fit into this. It was still hard to imagine Danil with family at all. He seemed like a mythical creature sprung from the sea, washed up on her beach. But he'd spoken of grandparents, of a missing father, a brother. Maybe his brother could help? "Who's your brother?"

His mouth firmed as if dealing with an unpleasant truth. "Aras. King of Gintaras."

Your future husband.

It had never occurred to her that this king might be… But that meant… "I don't understand. You're… a prince?"

"No. Aras is my half brother. Son of the old King and Queen. I am the previous king's bastard. The old king wanted me dead. Aras intervened." Danil spoke with no inflection, his dark eyes focused on the water.

Elsebet tried to keep up with this new information, but it made her feel…winded. This man had touched her intimately. She had… Suddenly marrying this *king* to keep Danil safe was more complicated. "I… would be your brother's wife?"

A muscle in his jaw ticked. He gave a sharp nod and did not meet her gaze. When he spoke, his voice was very quiet, almost impossible to hear over the swoosh of waves and wind. "If we move forward, you would be." He looked down at her then, gaze inscrutable. But he *looked* at her and that was something. "But this does not have to be the end result. There are…options."

She wanted to grab on to any and every option that wasn't marrying his *brother*, but she understood too well. If there hadn't been options *before* last night, why would there be any now? Unless they weren't *true* options. "Are any of them safe?"

He looked back out at the sea. "Quite safe."

"Safe for *you*?"

For a moment he was very quiet, and there was only the sound of the ocean. Such a strange still ness as everything rocked in the waves. "I am *The Weapon*, Elsebet."

"I do not like that nickname at *all*."

"It is apt. I may be the son of a king, but there is nothing royal or honorable about me. I have lived in dungeons. I have protected my brother with my own bare hands, not caring who I hurt in the process. I *am* a weapon for the crown of Gintaras, as befitting my station."

"Shouldn't your station be prince if you are the son of a king?"

"Bastard of the King."

Elsebet sighed heavily. "Honestly, royalty is forever complicating things."

For a moment, the briefest second, his mouth curved. He reminded her of the man he'd been at the dinners back at her castle. Never relaxed or *easy* exactly, no matter how he pretended, but someone who could amuse and be amused. Someone who could find joy in life, like when he'd teased her about doing chores. That simple but warm and caring life.

"On that we can agree." Then he sighed and the tiny smile was gone. "I will have to keep you locked in the room for the time being. I wanted to give you a moment of fresh air, of *this*. If the weather holds and all is well, we should be in Gintaras in two days. I will bring you out for walks around the deck as I am able, but you must act like someone put out by me. Peet will bring you your meals."

"What happens when we arrive in Gintaras?"

He was silent for long, stretched-out minutes that

had Elsebet holding her breath. She knew there was much she didn't know about him, but she understood parts of him. She could all but see his brain working.

He considered what he'd done last night a betrayal to his brother, and yet, he cared for *her* in some way. He would not betray them both. He'd tried to betray her, and he had not been able to fully bring himself to do it. Perhaps last night he'd even attempted to betray his brother, or been tempted to, but he had not. Not fully.

He would find some way to make this right on both sides. How, she did not know, but she pondered what she would do if she was in a similar position. If she had to choose between hurting Danil and hurting her little family back on the island, which would she pick?

She would sacrifice herself first, for those she cared about, for those she owed.

"Fear not, Princess," he said, confidently. "I will handle everything."

But he did not smile, and she found all she could do was *fear*.

Not this king or her future, but what Danil would now do to save her from the fate he himself had assigned her to. And how little a say she would have in it.

Danil did not trust himself to be alone with Elsebet for long. Neither did he trust Riks's eagle eyes on him at all times. There was something predatory about the way his brother's staff member watched him with such *ferocity*. All would be reported back to Aras, and this would normally be quite fine.

But it felt…bigger. Was that Elsebet's influence? Something to do with Riks? He could not determine. So he stayed out of his own chambers where Elsebet was kept, only venturing there to take her out on a walk for fresh air. These moments he could not resist giving her.

Every single time she ascended the stairs and the ocean came into view, her breath caught, her eyes widened. Every *single* time, there'd be a moment at the top of the stairs where she was completely and utterly still, taking it all in. Then she'd let her breath out, a long, slow sigh. And she would smile broadly and brightly.

He had known in his bones that it would affect her this way. He could not say how. Just that the ocean always had the same effect on him. No matter what swirled dark and edgy inside of him, the vast, sparkling blue always settled him like nothing else ever did.

Except the blue of her eyes. Which was what he watched now, every time. No longer the vast ocean and sky, but the way she lit up. A yearning fulfilled.

He had given that to her and wanted so badly to fulfill every want. Forever.

Because he had seen her gaze at the entrance to her cove with yearning and he had known she would feel the awe and amazement he felt in the middle of the ocean.

But he could not let the moments linger. No doubt

Riks had suspicions. This would not help Danil's cause. He had not figured out how to approach the problem of his brother and was running out of time, but the closer they got to Gintaras the more he knew he could not hand Elsebet over to Aras.

She might go willingly to save him—some miracle he still did not understand—but he could see, as if it had already happened, how easily his sharp-edged brother would damage her. He had been talking himself out of that from the beginning, but the more reality threatened, the less he could believe his own lies.

Danil could not allow her to be part of Aras's court of meanness and harsh punishments and cold isolation. A place where her soft, wonderful feelings would be punished—even worse than he believed they already had been by her father.

Danil needed a plan. Every walk along the ship's railing cemented this to him. Every moment of sailing the ship alongside Peet made him wonder how he would, for the first time in his life, refuse his duty.

"If the weather holds, we should be in Gintaras by the end of tomorrow," Peet said eagerly that afternoon, after Danil had left Elsebet back in her room following their walk. "Everyone will be eager to see you succeed."

Danil knew it was no success, but that nagging feeling he had that Riks was analyzing his every move kept him pretending all was well. "Was there any doubt?" he returned, offering Peet a smile.

But Riks clearly did not think this was amusing in any light. His pinched face got even grayer. "We thought you were dead. They even got rid of your things." He laughed to himself as if this was funny.

Neither Danil nor Peet joined in.

"Not to mention, when we learned of your survival the King did say to kill you if you didn't have her." Riks smirked, clearly irritated they did not find him amusing. "So I suppose there was *some* doubt."

Danil turned his gaze from the sea to Riks. He stared at the smaller man with a fierceness that must have been terrifying, because Riks—even with all his self-important posturing—shrank back.

Surely *kill* was an exaggeration, a figure of speech? Aras had *saved* him. Why would he turn around and…

But Riks, for all his cowering, did not relent. "It would have been right," he insisted in a voice that had gone up an octave. He was clearly scared of Danil's reaction. "The proper punishment for a failure of that magnitude. The King wants the Princess of Mathav, and so he shall have her."

Normally, Danil would have agreed with him. Aras was exacting. He had put men to death before for their failures, but…

Aras had *saved* Danil from death. They were brothers. Family. And family *cared*. It did not…punish failure with death.

He wanted to shake this thought away because it was foolish. They were not family in *that* sense. Danil was a bastard. Not as important. A tool to serve Aras, because of Aras's goodwill. Just as he had been a tool used by his mother's husband for his own gains. This was what he was *meant* for.

Any thoughts of care and family were just figments of his imagination. Some strange side effect of his injuries. Or...

Elsebet. For the first time in his life he had watched what a true family might look like. Or, worse, he'd been reminded. Although his childhood had been complicated, he *had* been a part of dinners like the ones Elsebet and her little family had, before his mother had married *that* man. Everyone helping, all shoved together in a table. His mother and grandparents sacrificing to make sure he had enough to eat.

He had set those memories aside. In a different part of his life, but Elsebet had reminded him, and worse, shown him it did not have to have anything to do with blood. She had treated her staff like family, and vice versa. She had gifted him her smiles, caring for him after he'd betrayed her.

If he hadn't met her, he would agree with Riks's assessment. That he should be put to death for failure to serve the King. It would not feel it like a blow. Like betrayal.

Why wouldn't his failure be punishable by death? Simply because he was the King's bastard brother? Foolishness. He knew his place.

And yet... Even as he let the conversation go, he could not let the *feelings* combating inside of him go. This was not what family did. And ever since Aras had saved him from that dungeon, the King had insisted they were *family*. That Aras had looked out for him, so Danil needed to do the same.

This was brotherhood. The only kind Danil had ever known.

But he thought of small, beautiful Elsebet yelling at rocks so as not to make her staff feel bad about her being upset. He thought of all the ways Nielson had tried to protect her from the likes of *him*. Without ever hurting Elsebet in the process. *That* was care, brotherhood. *That* was looking out for one another.

No threats of violence, death or betrayal involved. And he wanted to believe it was different because she was a woman, a princess. He was a bastard, a servant.

But he could not fully believe it after enjoying the warmth of their dinner table.

After Riks went to bed for the night, Danil could still not let it go. He looked at the stars above and then asked the simple question of Peet. "Is it true?"

Peet did not meet Danil's gaze, nor did he pretend to not understand what Danil asked. He frowned at the moon. "Riks is the King's man. Not me. I am a member of *your* guard. *Your* crew."

Which only meant Danil was his direct boss, but they both still served the King. And if Peet was on this ship and mission with Riks, he would have to know something of Aras's instructions. "But you would have received the orders to kill me, because we all know Riks could not kill me on his own. Even if he knew the right end of a gun."

Peet darted a glance at him then, but quickly looked away. "I knew you would not fail. You are *The*

Weapon. But more than that, sir, you are our leader. The King may be in charge, but your sailors and your soldier guards follow you because *you* are..." Peet trailed off a little, almost as if he was embarrassed. "You made a crew and army out of us, sir. Many of us appreciate that above all else."

But it was not an answer. Certainly not the one Danil wanted. Even if it warmed him in these old, shut-up spaces. That he might have made a crew, an army. Those weren't families, but they were...close.

Danil studied the starry sky above him. He wanted Elsebet to see it before they got close enough to land where the city lights would diminish all the sky offered. The vastness of the night. The brightness of the stars. Like her little island but supercharged out here in the middle of nowhere. No monarchies or royals or lands to fight for.

Only the water. Only the sky.

For a moment that stole his very breath, he wished that this was all there was. His ship, this ocean and her. No countries, no brothers, no duty.

When his entire life had been dedicated to *duty* because that was simple. That was accomplishable. All else was complicated. All else twisted and tore at his heart until it was impossible to breathe.

But duty... Duty was simple. Or had been.

Now there was Elsebet and nothing was simple anymore. So no, there was more than just this ship and this ocean and her. And he had to be strong enough to put her first. To make certain she was safe above all else.

Death was on the table if he faced down his brother and refused to give him Elsebet. And no amount of feeling betrayed by that knowledge changed the fact.

He thought of Elsebet. His sweet little siren. Who had forgiven him for his betrayal. No punishment necessary. Because she understood him. Cared for *him*. The way she cared for all those she loved. His selfless princess.

He would face down death before he let her sacrifice herself for the likes of *him*. Or anyone for that matter.

His duty had changed, here in the open sea where he thought best and was most himself. His duty was to her and her alone.

And if he died doing it, it would be worth the pain.

CHAPTER TWELVE

ELSEBET WAS EXCELLENT at isolation, or so she'd thought. Being locked up in this little room on this ship was its own kind of torture now that she'd seen what was outside. The sea, the sky. Like everything she'd dreamed about, but real. *Freedom*.

And Danil, always by her side while she took it all in. She could forget everything out in the vastness of it all, but here in this tiny room, she had nothing to do but *think*.

She worried about home. Nielson, Win, Inga. They would be so upset over this. She even worried about her father to an extent, though it was hard not to put some blame on him for this predicament she found herself in.

Which wasn't fair, since she couldn't seem to blame Danil for anything. Because duty was complicated, and she knew this too well to hold on to her anger over his kidnapping her.

Danil was in a state of conflict, and she so wished she could help ease it. The idea of marrying his brother… It filled her with more than the sort of beat-down acceptance she'd learned to embrace when it came to her future political marriage. She *recoiled* at the notion of marrying his *brother*.

She would have to forget that this king was connected to Danil. Put Danil aside. Forever. A stranger would not matter, or so it seemed. But Danil's *brother*?

Elsebet would do anything to save Danil and yet she did not know how to wrap her mind around this eventuality.

The door eased open, in Danil's careful way. She had not expected him again today as she knew it was getting late and thus far all their walks on the deck had been during the day. But he did the same thing he always did. Stood by the door. Held out his hand and said, "Come."

And every time, she did. Crossed to him, took his hand, and let him lead her up to the top of the ship in utter silence. She knew part of this silence was due to the King's man he did not trust and so did not want Riks overhearing anything, but part of it was him. Even with his voice healed, he did not need to chatter on like she had always liked to do on their walks on the beach.

Until he'd brought her here. Because now she too held her tongue. Every word she did utter felt... weighted, dangerous, filled with portent. But she forgot all those negative feelings as he led her up the stairs and into the dark.

Dark but not dark, because the night was clear and sparkling. She had always loved looking up on the beach at night, but it was not like this. Even the ceiling windows in her art studio were not like this. The sky seemed to *pulse*. Those stars and moon that had seemed like fixed beings on solid land were more like their own entities now. Moving and swirling.

"Danil…"

He squeezed her hand. A silent sort of *I know it is amazing*. "I thought you should see it before we get any closer to land," he said quietly.

They were getting closer to Gintaras. Every day. Every hour. And then what? She had said she would marry his brother to save him from whatever punishment awaited him, but… The reality of that was a panic beating in her chest.

She could not let him see that. Luckily it was dark. But she could not quite keep the words or the yearning inside. "I wish we could just stay right here forever."

He pulled her closer, until she was leaning against his chest and his arms were around her. He rested his chin on the top of her head and for moments of silence aside from the lapping of waves against the boat and the faint hum of engine they stood like this, watching the stars pulse.

He did not say a word. While he was not a talker as she was, something was still odd. The way he held her, so gentle. The way he said nothing, just looked at the stars. It all felt…tense, even though it should be a wonderful moment of peace before so much happened.

But maybe that was it. Something would happen

and soon and there would be no peace. But he had not done this—held her, watched the stars quietly with her—the entire time they'd been on his ship. It was as though something had changed, though she could not imagine what.

"Has something happened? You seem…" She searched for the right word. It wasn't the tenseness or the leashed darkness. These things were all part of him. Not even the grimness was different. But something lurked in the way he held her that was off.

It felt like goodbye.

But when he spoke it was not words of goodbye. It was a simple question.

"If you refused to do your duty, and your father could not simply force you to do it anyway, how do you think he would react?"

Elsebet was tempted to laugh such a question off since she had no power, but he seemed so very serious. So in need of a truthful answer. She considered it. "It is hard to say. Any time I have pushed back at what he wanted me to do, he tends to just wave it away as though I don't know what I'm talking about. Assures me it is the right course of action. Sends me away so I don't burden him with my feelings on the matter. If I flat-out refused…"

Elsebet really tried to picture it. She had seen her father angry, but never raging. He didn't yell. Oh, maybe he'd raise his voice in frustration, but he did not lose his temper.

He was the King. He believed in moderating his emotions for his kingdom so that they could trust he would always make rational, careful decisions. Since there was one decision he had not been able to make when it came to more heirs.

Which was why he expected the same of her. Always. Or maybe she'd learned to expect it of herself. To ease some of his guilt.

But she thought more about Danil's question and said, "I suppose he would be very angry. There might be a punishment. I could certainly see him forcing me to marry the man he had chosen. Not out of anger, but out of the assumption that I did not know better."

And now a strange new world had opened up to her, after Danil had kidnapped her.

What did a world look like if she did not follow her father's instructions? She did not know. Because while she had often voiced *opinions*, she had never fully refused her father. She'd always let him sway her. Always been determined to do her duty. To *help* ease his pain.

Like the man holding her now. She twisted in his arms so she could better see his moonlit face. "Why do you ask, Danil?"

His expression was grave, and he did not meet her gaze. He stared at the dark sea beyond the rail. "You have…people who care for you on your island. A family of sorts. Do you think your father cares for you?"

She did not understand why he asked these questions, in that dark rasp that she was beginning to assume was his voice and not the result of his injuries. They were speaking of serious things and still that rasp sent a shiver of want and memory through her.

His hands. His mouth.

Focus, Elsebet. Did she think her father cared for her? "Yes. As much as he can, I suppose. It's complicated. You see, he loved my mother very much. Never remarried. Never… I know he wished for a male heir, but he could never bring himself to…handle that." She sighed, wishing she did not have to cast back and think about her father. She could never view him as the villain, even when she wanted to.

But so also with Danil, so maybe she was simply too softhearted, too foolish to hate the people she should. Maybe this would forever be her downfall. Never getting what she wanted as she served those who could not see her.

But Danil did. He'd shown her the ocean. She *knew* he was thinking of a way not to deliver her to his brother. Finding a way to *keep* her, rather than send her away. They shared a connection, even if neither knew how to put it into words. And she'd rather be here, in Danil's strong arms, conflicted and hurting, than stuck in that tiny room, or even her island castle and *hate* everyone. She'd gone through that phase too, and it didn't change anything.

Bitterness was no match for love. It felt…smarter to harden her heart, but it didn't *feel* better. It didn't feel *right*. She was starting to accept she'd rather feel love and warmth than worry about *smartness*. No matter how that might disappoint her father.

Maybe she would regret this someday, but she would always remember the way the stars pulsed above and Danil's heart beat under her palm.

"I look like my mother. I think part of my isolation was for my protection, but Nielson believed part of it was that it hurt to look at me." And it had made sense. Lived within her.

She was a bad memory. Or a good one, depending on how you looked at it. But as a young girl it had made her all that much more determined to make her father proud, happy. So he might look at her and see... Elsebet. Not the mother she'd never known. So he might not worry so much about *protection,* rather see her as a person. His daughter. Someone to share the duties of the Kingdom with, to be part of his life.

But whenever she'd tried to be herself, whenever she'd hurt or been angry, he'd shut her away, sent her off. Everything she was and felt was more burden to her father than bounty.

She'd spent the past few years hoping that if she married whomever her father wanted to, if she did her duty as the King asked, he might finally be able to look at her like he had when she'd been a child. As her own person, important in his eyes, and not as the ghost of her mother.

Elsebet sighed and leaned deeper into the warmth of Danil. "So, yes, I think he cares, but I think... It is not the way you might wish for a father to care. Did your mother care for you?"

"Complicated," he said gruffly.

"Tell me."

And to her surprise, he did. "I was raised by my mother and grandparents. I did not know who my father was. This suited us all well enough, though we were poor and struggling. But after my grandmother died, my grandfather's health faltered. Mother spent much time caring for him, as did I. When he died, it was as if we were...adrift. Without them, we had no anchor."

He took a careful breath, his gaze on the ocean. "Not long after, mother married. I believe she was searching for that anchor. Things became more difficult after this marriage. She told the man truths that she'd never told me. The King was my father. Her husband was a lazy sort, and he leaned on me to do most of the work for the family. But knowing I was royalty? He saw this as a ticket to riches. Then, so did my mother."

He spoke very coldly as he continued with the story. As if none of it mattered, but the fact he shared it with her at all proved it did. From the way his mother was swayed by this man, to being marched into the castle, to being thrown in a dungeon.

"Aras stood up for me. Saved me from our father's death sentence. When he became king, I became his most trusted guard. I would go on missions. My mother begged to see me, but I refused. I could not bring myself to forgive her. For putting that man above my safety. His needs above my own. So I did not see her. Refused. I returned from a mission for Aras with news she had died. An accident."

She heard the grief and guilt, even if he didn't voice the words. He blamed his mother, had been hurt by her, but these things did not erase love.

She understood this on a deep, enduring level. And

now that she had the full picture of him, she understood what had started these questions. "Are you afraid of your brother's reaction if you do not bring me to him?"

"According to Riks, if I did not have you, they were meant to kill me on the spot."

She sucked in a breath of shocked pain. *Kill* him? "I do not have siblings, but this is not the mark of family. Of love."

He was very quiet for a very long time. "Aras is the only one who has ever tried to protect me." His gaze turned to her then. "Until you."

That gaze, those words, shivered through her. *I will always protect you.* But she could not vow it out loud, because she now understood how much he risked even in this moment, because of Riks's prying eyes.

"I should go back to my room. You needn't accompany me."

But he held her still. "Elsebet."

She shook her head. "You should not risk yourself for me," she whispered fiercely. Because that was what he was doing by being out here with her. Telling her these things. Giving her a chance, a hope. Himself.

"What better thing would there be for me to risk myself for?" His hand swept over her hair, a gentle touch. Because for as large and rough as he was and could be, he had a well of gentleness inside of him he did not seem to know how to wield.

Except when it came to her.

"I had vowed I would never be in search of an anchor like my mother was, but you are my anchor, Elsebet. Vows or no." His mouth pressed to her temple. Her cheek. She should resist. Refuse. But his words were spoken roughly and with emotion. "Let me give you everything you want, Elsebet. My princess. My siren. Let me be yours."

It was that last sentence that swayed her. He did not wish her to be *his*—as was her only experience in the world. A belonging to be passed along. A pawn. A *thing*.

But no. He did not want to own her or possess her. He wished to *give himself.* To her. And this was all she wanted. Body. Soul.

And heart.

He kissed her there under the stars with the sounds of the ocean. Risk and Aras be damned. His entire life be damned.

For this was the one thing no one could turn against him. He had tried. Kidnapping her. Convinced he would deliver her to Aras.

And still she was here. Kissing him back with that warmth. Wanting to protect *him*, even after all he'd done to put her in danger's way.

It was painful, conflicting, but he could not deny her truth after having spent time on her little island. Violence was not what family did to one another. This was not love, or care.

Those things involved wanting to protect and giving the other person everything they desired. A complicated tightrope.

Elsebet held on to him, but she pulled her mouth away.

"Danil, if Riks sees…"

"Come." He moved her to the staircase and back down into the boat. Toward his quarters. Danil was quite certain Riks was fast asleep, eager to be back on solid land, but it did not matter. Danil found nothing at all mattered anymore except finding a way to keep Elsebet safe.

And his.

He ushered her back into his room as he always did. He usually left her at this point. No touch, no kiss, nothing that might give him away. Nothing that might change *everything*.

But everything *was* changed. He closed the door behind him and they stood staring at each other.

He cupped her perfect face in his hands. Stared into those midnight blue siren eyes. While something old swirled in him. Something he thought had died. Stronger than duty.

But he did not have the words for it. Not here.

She rose to her toes and pressed her mouth to his anyway. So he tried to pour his feelings, those storms into his kiss. They wrapped their arms around each other like anchors. Like they could survive the hurricanes that brewed within.

And without.

He knew they could not. Not together, but for this moment, he would have this together. He would be hers in all things. He slid his hands over her braid, her back, pulling down the zipper of her dress.

His body hardened, but he did not rush ahead. He lost himself in the scent of her, the silk of her skin. Carefully, intentionally, he rid her of all her clothes. Then his own. He shed his shirt, and she spread her fingers across the scarred skin of his chest before looking up at him. "This will not be like last time, Danil. I want all of you."

Their gazes met. He could refuse. It would give him some kind of plausible deniability when it came to Aras. A workaround when he faced down his powerful and dangerous brother.

But he did not want that. He did not want a loophole. He wanted his beautiful siren, and he would have her. Safe, whole, his. She would never suffer at the hands of another.

It would have to be goodbye. Maybe not forever. If he could get through to his brother, he would return to her. But he could not until he knew she would be safe, always, from Aras's wrath. If he could not protect her, her father would. And whatever happened to Danil himself would be a sacrifice he was willing to give her.

She had sacrificed for him. She had showed him what love truly was, or reminded him. Either way, she had awoken him from a long slumber. Breathed life into *The Weapon*.

She would be his for this, and he hers. And if it had to be enough, it would be.

So he kissed her, touched her, revered her. He

tasted every inch of her, until she shook, begged, was so gloriously, desperately his, naked underneath him. He took her to the peak, again and again, his name forever on her lips.

Until it was time. "It might hurt. I promise, only for a moment, but I cannot promise away the pain."

Her gaze met his. Hazy with desire, yes, but calm. Certain. And knowing. "Nor can I." Because she spoke of more than physical pain. She spoke of everything to come. They could not promise it would not hurt.

But he could protect her.

And he could give her this.

Perhaps he had lost his handle on everything. Perhaps this was selfishness and wrong. Perhaps...

He did not care. He was changed. By her smile. By her kindness. She had saved him, in all the ways there were.

And if he went to Gintaras and died by his brother's hand, this moment would be worth it.

Entering her, his beautiful, perfect siren. One with all she was. Freedom. The ocean. *Love*. All he'd ever yearned for, right here in her.

She sighed his name as if she too had been waiting for this, just this. No matter the discomfort, she accepted him, moved with him, until he could see that pleasure on her face once more, feel the force of her climax against him, bringing on his own.

The release was the biggest storm that had ever battered him. From somewhere so deep within he had not known it existed. She held on to him tightly as it raged through both of them, wrapped up together as they slowly, inch by inch, came back to reality.

She trailed her fingers down his back, and he nuzzled into her hair. He felt her heartbeat and for a moment simply basked in all that he had been given.

He knew he was destined to lose it, but that was okay. If she was safe forever, that was okay.

As if she could read his mind, she pulled away slightly. She sat up on her elbow, glaring down at him. "I will not forgive you if you let him hurt you."

She was so serious. Such a princess in this moment. This her royal decree.

"Then I will endeavor to survive, Your Highness." He smiled at her, a true smile that felt foreign on his lips. Only she had brought that smile out of him since he'd been a boy. He would cherish her forever for it.

"We will face Aras together. As a team. As a family," she said. Still ordering him about. Perhaps he should have been offended, but he liked the side of her that took charge.

Even if he could not allow it.

Family. A fairy-tale dream these days. She still believed, and he wanted to give her everything he believed.

He pulled her into the circle of his arms, brushed her hair off her face as she drifted into sleep. He waited in the dark, making his plan. To keep her safe. Always.

So, no. She would not be coming with him. They could not be a team in this.

Because he knew Aras. He would want to punish

Danil, yes. Kill him, probably, for what he'd done, even if he delivered Elsebet. She was no longer the untouched princess promised.

But Danil would not turn her over. He could not. Because Aras would not leave it at punishing Danil. He would not let Elsebet go unscathed. So Danil had to make certain she was safe above all else.

It was his fault she was in this mess at all. He could not let her be hurt because of it.

So this would have to be his goodbye. Temporary, hopefully, but if it had to be permanent, so be it.

CHAPTER THIRTEEN

WHEN ELSEBET WOKE, he was gone. Something like dread crept into her chest. But that was silly. He had slipped out before morning in order to avoid being found out. He was likely off doing something important with the boat. They would not have much time left before they arrived in Gintaras.

She knew Danil did not plan on turning her over to his brother. But she had told him they were a team, and she meant it. They would work together. She had spent her entire life being protected, and she could not stand the thought of him joining those ranks.

Surely he understood that. How important it was to stand together. To be equals. She was no pampered princess to be isolated away while *he* handled everything. He knew that.

Right?

She chewed her lip, wondering. He had not *disagreed* with her when she said they were a team, but he hadn't *confirmed* it either. He had not said, *Yes, Elsebet, we will confront Aras together.*

He'd said nothing.

Dread settled heavier and heavier, like an anchor on her chest.

She got dressed quickly and rushed to the stairway. As she breached the stairs, she saw land. Not far off. Shining buildings of a city. Unlike Mathav, the beaches looked quite welcoming and not rocky. Though the air was a brittle kind of cold she was used to. This was no tropical isle, that was certain.

Still, the only person she saw was the crew member who brought her meals. Peet was his name. He was doing something with ropes and… Elsebet watched as the shore seemed to get oddly…farther away.

She whirled to face Peet. "Where is Danil?" she demanded.

The man blinked at her. He had not spoken to her at all the entire time she'd been on the ship. He seemed to get tongue-tied and blushed a deep red. But she could tell he had a kind of hero worship toward Danil, so she did not worry about him.

She worried about Danil though. If he was not here, and they were moving *away* from shore. "Where is Danil? Answer me. *Now*."

"He's gone ashore, miss. Ma'am. Lady," he babbled, tacking on all sorts of honorifics. None of them correct.

She could not possibly care less.

"And what are you doing? Why are *we* not ashore?"

"Erm, well. Ma'am. That is, Your Highness." He bobbed a strange little bow.

"What are you doing?" she repeated through clenched teeth, her hands curled into fists. She was rarely tempted into violence, but this man's nonanswers were getting her there.

"I have my orders, miss. That is, Princess."

Orders. *Orders.* "Your orders are to turn around. To take me to Gintaras."

"Miss." Peet shook his head, hat squashed in his hands. "Do you know how much trouble I'll be in?"

"From *who*?"

"Danil, of course. The captain. He's ordered me to take you to Mathav. You'll be safe there. He's only trying to protect you."

Mathav.

It was a knife to the heart. Not just trying to protect her but sending her away. As her father had done. Always little more than a piece of property to be shucked about. She swallowed against the hard lump that formed in her throat.

It hurt, but that hurt did not take away the *fear*. Not only was Danil treating her like a pawn to be shipped away, but he was putting himself in danger. Alone.

"And if *I* am safe there, where will Danil be safe?" Elsebet demanded of the man. "Because I do not think it is on Gintaras without me. If he goes to his brother without me, what happens to *him*?"

Peet blinked a few times, mouth open but no words coming out.

"He is your captain, is he not? Do you wish him to *die*?"

"King Aras is his brother. I can't imagine he'd put Danil to death. Not really. I know he threatened it, but sometimes a threat is just a threat. Especially from King Aras. He's a bit of a hothead. That's all. They're brothers."

Elsebet almost felt sorry for the man, who looked more like a boy the more he spoke. She had thought the same once. But she knew Danil did not overreact. If he thought his brother might harm him for failing, the King surely would.

"I wish I believed this to be true, but I have my doubts. He is sending me away to keep me safe because *he* will not be safe." She wanted to damn him for such a stupid decision, but he was not *here.*

He's shipping you off so he doesn't have to deal with your theatrics when you do not get what you want.

It was her father's voice, frustrated and dismissive. He'd sent her away.

"He's only trying to protect you," Nielson had said, patting her hand as she'd cried on the boat to the island.

But he hadn't been. He'd been protecting his own bruised heart. And it wasn't that he didn't love her, and it wasn't that Danil didn't love her, but they did not know how to let their walls down to *see* her.

And now Danil was sending her away. Without him. So *he* could handle everything, and *she* could go have her emotional outburst elsewhere.

No.

"We must put a stop to this, Peet. We must not let him sacrifice himself."

"B but I don't think we should interfere," Peet said, trying to stand taller and puff out his chest. Poor boy trying to play at being a soldier. "He is *The Weapon*," Pete said, as if such a foolish nickname could make a man, flesh and blood, invincible.

"He is Danil Laurentius. He is a *man*, strong and good as that man may be." *Sending you off like a piece of sea glass*. She shoved that thought away for the time being. First, he had to survive, then she could be angry with him. "And from the sound of things, this King Aras is *not* good. If he was set to have Danil killed for failing to obtain me, how would he react if Danil tells him he has obtained me and then let me go? Not well, I would think. Turn the ship around and bring me to shore, Peet."

Peet's expression grew more and more unsure. "But…what can *you* do?"

Elsebet lifted her chin, fixed him with the harsh royal glare she had learned at her father's knee. "I am the Princess of Mathav. I will do what I must." *This* was her duty. And she would not let anyone take it from her.

Even Danil.

Danil was not nervous. He might not know what waited for him, but he knew that he was right. That Elsebet was safe.

These were the only two things that mattered. He felt that, all the way through the morning. Walking into the castle. Being asked to wait—naturally. Aras always liked to play his games.

Then, when he was summoned, it was not to Aras's

office or parlor, but the grand hall. Where Aras's court was arranged like this was some grand event.

Or trial.

Danil walked slowly up the aisle, his gaze never wavering from his brother on the throne. Danil knew he still *looked* injured, and perhaps a few more days at sea would have returned more strength to him, but these thoughts were irrelevant.

He was here to set Elsebet free, and so she would be.

He had walked this road before, though always after a success that Aras had deemed not *quite* successful enough. Those times he had been filled with shame, the desire to do better for the man who had saved his life.

Danil felt no shame now. He felt like an entirely different person. And it was a strange feeling to walk the same path, face the same people, and see it from all new eyes, when he'd been certain, only a few weeks ago, that he was *The Weapon* and he would bring back his cargo.

But being shipwrecked, being taken in by Elsebet and her makeshift family, had changed everything he'd known. People were not cargo. They were not weapons.

And Aras was no family. He was no different than Danil's mother's husband. Out for himself. Out for power.

Meanwhile, somewhere on a strange little island, three people were no doubt worried sick about the woman they all loved. As they'd worry for a daughter, though she was a princess and they were her subjects.

Danil knew he did this for them, and the kindness they'd shown him, as much as he did this for Elsebet. Peet would not return her to them right now. It was too dangerous with Aras knowing where she was, and that small trio not strong enough to fight whomever Aras might send.

So Peet would take Elsebet to her father. Mathav might not have a strong army, but they would protect their princess.

And if he marries her off to some other king or prince in the meantime?

Danil could not concern himself with this. If she was alive, not married to his cruel brother, this was all that mattered. If he lived to tell the tale, he would stop whatever, save her in whatever way. If he did not, he had left Peet instructions.

"So. You have returned empty-handed."

Danil looked up at his brother, lounging in his throne, looking cold as ice, but Danil knew that was a lie.

He was enraged. "Where is my man?" Aras asked, his fingers dancing over the jewels in the scepter he held like some sort of dragon in love with his riches.

Maybe he was, and Danil was no prince, but he would save the Princess all the same.

"He will be returned to you," Danil replied, trying not to smile. Because he had dropped Riks off at Piyer, a small island used in the summer for swimming larks. In the winter, basically isolated and cold.

He would suffer for a few hours, and then Danil or Aras would send someone to fetch him. "When I see fit."

Aras eyed him, dark eyes that Danil had always seen as the same, but now they were cold. Detached. "You have gotten quite big for your britches, *brother*. A man who shipwrecks, nearly dies, and then returns without his cargo should not be quite so confident, I wouldn't think."

Yes, love will do that to you.

"Things have changed."

"I hope this is the head injury speaking." Aras glanced back at his court members, who laughed. On command.

So many things given to Aras on command. And how was Aras different from their father? Danil had always considered him good because, well, if the old king had survived, would Danil be alive? No.

But now he wondered. Was it simple enough to save someone, or did it require more to love? More, he thought. Much more. "How do you rule differently than your father, Aras?"

"I do not know what has come over you, *Weapon*, but this is not the topic at hand. Where is my princess, and how do you dare return to me without her?"

Danil moved up the stairs—where he was very much not allowed. He watched as Aras fidgeted in his chair, flicking a glance at the soldiers who lined the walls.

The soldiers did not meet Aras's furtive glances.

They watched Danil. Because, as head of the King's Guard, Danil was in charge of them. Not the King.

An interesting realization. Reminding him of Peet's words. That his sailors and soldiers were loyal to *him*, because he'd brought them together. Made them a unit.

Something like a family.

Danil kept walking. Past the normal point where he would stop and bow to his brother. Instead, he walked right up to the throne.

Aras's eyes widened. "Guards!"

But Danil held up a hand. A signal to *his* men, not to draw their weapons or move. But to stay put.

They stayed put.

"*I* am the head of the King's Guard, if you re-call," Danil said, and this time he *did* smile. He was surprised, at first, to see the fear in the eyes of his brother and the court members, but in a strange way it all made sense.

They were weak. Ruling with manipulation and *weapons*, but not their own strength. Unless order-ing people to the dungeons was power. When they did not have their weapons to do their bidding…they were just scared weaklings.

As a young man, Danil had thought command-ing people was power. But now he knew. Power was in protecting those you loved. And those who had no power.

Aras had no love. And he had no true power.

"The Princess of Mathav is not yours to have, Aras. Now, you can accept this, or you can make it difficult. The choice is yours, but the result will not change."

Aras's eyes narrowed. He was clearly working on banking that fear, on figuring out a new tactic to put Danil under his thumb, but Danil would not go. He would not give in.

He was a changed man. And in that change, whatever power Aras had once held over him was gone. Splintered and lost, like his beloved ship.

"You think you have a say here, *Weapon*? You are mistaken. I will find her. Guards, arrest this man!" When no one made a move to do anything, Aras smashed his scepter against the ground. "*I* am your king."

There were some shared glances among the guards. Silent conversations among brothers not of blood but of missions. Of hard training. Of a common purpose. To serve and protect Gintaras.

Danil understood these men, had trained these men. They were conflicted because they had taken oaths. But those oaths had been to Gintaras.

Not a spoiled child of a king.

Danil turned his back on Aras—a great offense—and addressed the guards lined up, fidgeting, unsure what to do. "Men. Brothers. You have a choice here. You may in fact follow the King. If you think he is right. If you think Gintaras will succeed with his rule, I encourage you to protect him above all else. Arrest me, if you must."

"And if we don't?" Corbel, one of the veteran guards that Danil had always thought would be a good replacement for him should he ever perish in a mission, asked.

"Then you may follow me, my brothers."

"*I* am your brother."

Danil turned slowly to face Aras. "No. I thought you were, but you have only ever seen me as a tool. Your *weapon*. This is not a brotherhood, Aras."

"You have no choice! I am your king!" Aras stood, waving his scepter wildly at the guards. "If you do not arrest him, all of you will be in the dungeons!"

Danil felt foolish and a bit disgusted with himself for ever feeling swayed by this man. But that was what a crumb of light could do in years of darkness.

Elsebet, luckily, was no crumb. She was the entire sun, and she made him see this for what it really was.

Even Aras's court looked embarrassed.

"I resign as your weapon, Aras. I have no desire to be part of the King's Guard. I am leaving Gintaras." He looked at the guardsmen who lined the walls. "Whoever wishes to come with me may meet me in port by noon."

"I will have you killed!" Aras shouted.

Danil began walking away. He didn't even look at the man who'd claimed to be his brother but hadn't cared at all. "By whom and with what army, Aras?"

Danil left the castle and did not look back. He headed for the docks, where he had three more ships. He also had two ships in other ports, and he would need to collect those as well.

This was not over—Aras still had riches and allies. But without his guards it would take time to mass an offensive.

In the meantime, Elsebet would be safe with her father. And Danil… He was not worthy of any princess, but he could be her protector. Go to Mathav and dedicate his life to her. Ensure that she did not have to follow any of her father's proclamations.

Thanks to his siren, he was free, and he would spend the rest of his life ensuring that she was as well.

CHAPTER FOURTEEN

ELSEBET STOOD ON the deck of the ship, leaning against the railing, impatiently waiting for Peet to anchor the boat at the dock. It was a pretty morning in Gintaras, but her mood was black.

He's only trying to protect you.

How many times had she heard that in her life? And yes, she had been protected, but she had also never been seen in all that protecting. She had thought Danil was different.

He was not.

Once the boat was *finally* secure, Peet began to lower a ramp onto the dock. At a snail's pace. Elsebet waited, trying very hard not to tap her toe. She scowled at Peet, who was clearly taking his sweet time, as if that would change anything.

He'd brought her back to shore, hadn't he?

Once the ramp was firmly in place, she sailed past him and down it onto the dock. It was bustling with people and Elsebet did not know where she was going. This was not like the island or Mathav, where the castle was immediately visible from shore. How far would she need to go to reach it? How would she find it without help?

Oh, damn every man.

She turned back to Peet to ask him, but he was wringing his hands from the deck of the boat, looking out at the crowd. She heard something, a commotion of sorts, and turned toward it.

There he was. She was so angry at him and still her heart soared. Danil was unscathed. Whole and perfect. And she couldn't help but realize some of her anger had been in an attempt to blank away the fear that his brother would hurt him because of her.

But no. He was whole and here. She might have forgotten herself and run to him, but his expression was furious as he stormed toward them. "What the hell are you doing here?" he yelled.

But all that anger, the yelling, was directed at Peet up on the boat. As if she didn't even exist. And she was angry all over again.

She lifted her chin and tried to pin him with a hard gaze while he didn't even *look* at her. "I told Peet to turn around."

Danil turned angry eyes on her. "For what purpose? To throw yourself in the midst of danger?"

"You have. Why should I not?"

"Because I am a king's guard. Well versed in battle, pain and punishment. And you are a pampered princess who cannot follow simple instructions."

The words pierced deep, where she already felt soft and vulnerable. *Stay away, Elsebet, you are not wanted.*

"You have left me no instructions, Danil. You just *left*." She would not let her eyes fill or her mouth waver at that, at the possibility that was what hurt most of all. Him sneaking away with no goodbye. Throwing her back to her father like she was an unwanted fish.

"We do not have time for this," he muttered, taking her by the arm and steering her back up the ramp onto the boat. "I have left my brother's employ. I have renounced my citizenship. Many of the King's guards are coming with me. We will escort you back to Mathav. Any of my men who wish it may pledge allegiance to you or your father, helping Mathav's military weaknesses somewhat."

She pulled her arm out of his grasp at the top of the ramp. "Did it occur to you to ask what *I* wanted?"

He frowned down at her, clearly beyond confused. "I have taken care of everything. You will be protected and safe."

"Because I am incapable?"

"Elsebet."

"What if I wanted to go back to the island? What if I wanted to go away from *all* these places? Who are you to determine I am to be returned to my father?"

His eyebrows drew together, his mouth a firm, harsh line. "You are lucky it was I who kidnapped you. Not everyone would see the error of their ways. Not everyone would return you at all."

"Lucky?" She might have screamed it, that was how much of a slap it was. *Lucky*. As if any of this was *luck*.

"We will return to Mathav. I have taken care of Aras, but he may buy himself another army at some point. He will never forgive me for my betrayal, but worse, he will insist on breaking the toy he could not have. So, Elsebet, we will do as *I* say."

"Perhaps I can protect myself."

Danil laughed. *Laughed.* She curled her hands into fists. She did not use them on him, though it was *tempting.* Still, she whirled away from him. "Peet?"

"Yes, Miss Highness?"

"I would like you to take me back to my island. I will pay you handsomely. But Danil Laurentius is not allowed on this boat."

"But it's his boat, ma'am."

"I'll buy it."

Danil's voice was a growl. "No, you will not."

Elsebet shot him a hard look. "I'm not talking to you, Danil."

"You are talking about *my* boat, and Peet has no leave to sell it."

"Do you have a boat yourself, Peet? Or know someone who does?"

The poor man was the color of a tomato, fidgeting and uncomfortable as he looked from Danil to Elsebet. "Erm."

"Fine. You're of no use. I'll go find someone who *is* of use." She strode down the ramp toward the crowd, which was mostly paying them no attention except for a growing number of men with their uniforms and weapons, who must be soldiers. She didn't care. She would storm down the entire dock until she found someone who would sail her home. Not Mathav. *Home*.

And then, just as she had been back on a beach days ago, she was suddenly in Danil's arms. Bouncing against his shoulder as he carried her onto his boat. This time it wasn't shock that kept her from screaming or hitting him, it was the *crowd*. She could see *many* curious eyes on her now.

He shouted out orders to different soldiers. Some on this ship, some on that ship. All the while he carried her across the deck of the ship, directing Peet to cast out to sea once more.

When he finally set her on her feet, she was seething with rage. But instead of like the *last* time he'd manhandled her onto the boat, there was no stoic response. No guilt. There was only her own anger turned back at her.

"This was wrong of you, Elsebet. Did I not make it clear how dangerous my brother is?"

"And yet here you are unscathed, while I was meant to be shipped off. To what? Never see you again?"

Some shock worked through that fury on his face, but not enough. "I was going to follow you to Mathav, Elsebet. Once I knew my brother could not be a threat."

"And I was supposed to know this how?"

"Trust?"

"Trust? You are a kidnapper!"

Everything in his expression cooled. From heat

to ice. And she shivered, her heart a painful ache in her chest.

"Perhaps by the time we arrive in Mathav, you will have calmed yourself and understand that I will always protect you, no matter how little you like it."

Calmed yourself. Because this was always it, was it not? She could not hold in all those swirling emotions and she had to be sent away. Until she was calm. Until she could be *used.*

Never was she meant to just be a *part* of some-one's life. "Protect me?" she said, trying to be that *calm* everyone so desperately wanted. "By carrying me onto ships and taking me places against my will?"

"If your will is flawed."

All attempt at calm evaporated. She narrowed her eyes at him, moved forward with her finger pointed. She jabbed it into his chest but was met with only the hard wall of him. "When we arrive in Mathav, I will have you…" Her anger wilted. She had been about to say thrown in jail. But that was what his brother had done to him, and even in her anger she could not say it.

But she could see in his expression that he knew exactly what she'd meant to say, and it made her feel worse than she already did.

"You have wronged me. Twice," she said, willing the crack out of her voice.

"Yes, you punished me so the first time by invit-ing me into your bed."

It burned because it was true. She'd been mad at

him for all of five minutes before he'd twisted her heart into knots.

Well, not this time. This time she was determined.

Except the whole part where she was desperately, irrevocably in love with him. With his honor.

He did not see her, did not value…who she was. This should make all that love evaporate.

But it didn't.

"You should have asked," she said, and she was calm, though tears leaked through. She would not sob, she would not create a dramatic scene again so he'd have even stronger reason to send her away.

But she couldn't help the crying part as she said the rest, holding his gaze. "You, of all people, should have treated me as a person instead of cargo. You have heard me speak of feeling as though I am nothing but a pawn, and yet you have chosen to make me one. Again and again."

He looked stricken, and that made her hurt. When she *wanted* him to be stricken. She wanted him to understand. And yet…she couldn't watch. It made her want to reach out and soothe.

So she turned away from him and went into the room. Her prison. She shut the door quietly behind her. Right in his face.

Danil brooded. The stars shone above, making his mood all the more foul. Because Elsebet was in her room. Refusing to speak with him.

He *should* take her to Mathav. It was foolish to give in to her wants. He needed to protect her.

Perhaps I can protect myself.

He hadn't ordered Peet to change course yet. They were still on course to make it to Mathav the next day.

But the island weighed on his mind. Elsebet's words weighed on his mind. The hurt look in her eyes. Those words, in an echo of surround sound.

You, of all people, should have treated me as a person instead of cargo. You have heard me speak of feeling as though I am nothing but a pawn, and yet you have chosen to make me one. Again and again.

A pawn. He of course did not see her as one, but he could not make an argument for his behavior. He had kidnapped her twice. And right now, if he didn't tell Peet to change course before midnight, he would take her where she did not wish to go.

You should have asked.

Danil sighed. He could not risk the sail into the cove. Not with her on the boat. Not with what had happened last time. But Peet could drop them off at the edge of the island again. That *would* be safer.

Giving her what she wanted was not smart, though. Her little staff could hardly protect her if—no, *when*—Aras found someone brave enough to sail there.

He was only trying to *save* her.

You should have asked.

Frustrated by these rotating thoughts, Danil forced himself into the captain's room, where Peet watched the instruments that led them toward Mathav.

Peet looked up. Surveyed him. "Change of plans?"

Hell. "Not just yet, but be ready. I..." He had always been honest with his staff, his soldiers. Straight with them, because that was how loyalty was built. But he didn't often let his *emotions* get in the way of that. It had always felt like a weakness. His men looked up to him to be *The Weapon*.

But he had hardly been that on this return voyage, and still here Peet was. With no promise of payment or return to his home. As though loyalty mattered more than what he'd made himself into.

And Elsebet made it seem like feelings, emotions, honesty and vulnerability...these things had power. "I should ask her what she wishes."

Peet took in this information, nodding thoughtfully. "She's a bit scary when she's in a lather."

Danil chuckled. Not the word he'd use, but he understood. She was beautiful when angry. Such a force. But she didn't wield it all the time. She used her smile. Her kindness. The way she saw people.

She had anger and fury in her, but she did not use it as a weapon unless pushed to the brink. As he'd done to her.

He should take her to her father and wash his hands of this failed experiment.

"She feels I have behaved wrongly. Going to speak to my brother, returning her to her father, without asking what she wanted." Danil still wasn't *fully* convinced, because of course he knew the right course of action.

But maybe what would make her happy wasn't so much his *doing* the thing she wanted as caring enough to ask? Having a discussion?

He thought of that evening at her kitchen table on

the island. When they'd spoken of the cracked window high above, and Nielson's fear of heights. How Elsebet had said she would handle it. Because she *knew*.

And so Danil also *knew*. What he should do. How to protect her.

You should have asked.

He heaved out another sigh.

"It seems she's probably right," Peet offered. "The way my mother tells it, women usually are."

But she was *wrong*. To land on Gintaras. To want to go back to her island unprotected. "How can she expect to protect herself when she has never once had to? Answer me that."

Peet took some time to consider this, staring thoughtfully out the darkened window. "Maybe you should teach her. Before they married, my sister taught her husband how to dance for some event he had, and he fell head over heels. Now she's about to have my *third* niece." Peet shook his head with some disapproval.

"It is not so simple with a princess and a bastard, Peet."

"You *are* a king's son. Even if not a queen's." Peet shrugged, as if the bastard part held no weight. "You have been the head of the King's Guard for quite some years and inspired such confidence and loyalty that they follow you. Away from their king and country, because they know. You are the noble one."

Danil was surprised at Peet's simple response. As if it was obvious to anyone with eyes that Danil was worthy. When…surely no one else would think that. Not the King of Mathav when it came to his daughter.

"It doesn't hurt to ask for permission," Peet continued. "I rather think you're a charming couple."

Again Danil wanted to laugh, but the sound caught in his throat. He could admit to himself, in the privacy of his own mind, that he loved Elsebet. Everything she was. And he knew he was strong, an impeccable soldier. He had much to offer many.

But not a *princess*. Any request to her father would no doubt end with refusal. "He will say no."

"You've fought your own brother for her. I do not know why you wouldn't fight her father too."

Danil looked at the man who had been with him on many a mission. Who was not a leader, but a good man. Always willing to do his *duty*. And in this moment, not afraid of the truth as he saw it.

"You are very wise, Peet."

Peet chuckled. "Name your firstborn after me as tribute, sir."

Firstborn. What a strange thought. Curling around him like dread…but not that, because it was lighter.

Hope, he realized. A feeling that seemed foreign now, but he had felt it once. It had died when his mother had married, when his childhood had changed, when he'd become a tool. And then *The Weapon*.

And now there was Elsebet, who had warmed him from the inside out. Melting those old protections until he felt as unsure as a boy. As unprotected as any newborn.

"I will keep course to Mathav for the time being, sir, but we can always change course. Whenever you're ready."

Danil nodded. "You are a good man, Peet."

Peet offered a little salute and Danil turned. Elsebet was not *right* about what she wanted to do, but she was not *wrong* about how he had handled it poorly.

And yet what future was there for them? A princess and a warrior? He could hardly promise one or ask for one. She cared too much for her father, her kingdom.

And he cared too much for her.

Perhaps the lesson was simple enough. Instead of just deciding…he needed to ask. Which went against *everything* he'd turned himself into as *The Weapon*. Do not ask. Do not worry. Act, do. Accomplish.

But he was no longer *The Weapon*.

CHAPTER FIFTEEN

ELSEBET LIKED TO think she'd calmed down. Found a rational, reasonable center. She had made an error. Thinking Danil, or *any* man, could see beyond their own noses—or other appendages—to see women as anything other than property to be hefted about.

That was fine. She would dedicate her life to a convent, perhaps. Learn how to pray away her feelings.

She sat on the bed, cross-legged, chin in her hands, and cursed herself for a fool.

Men or convent, neither choice really gave her comfort. Or solved what ached and swirled within her, an annoying, heavy conflict.

When a knock sounded on her door, her heart soared, even as that heavy conflict grew barbs and settled on her heart. Impossible situations with impossible answers.

Danil did not slip inside the room as he had these nights past. No. He waited. Because he hadn't locked her in this time. She had locked *herself* in. She scowled and got off the bed, opening the door.

He stood there, looking stiff and stoic, hands

linked behind his back like some sort of soldier. And he was a soldier, there was no doubt about that.

"I would like to have a discussion," he said, and before she could tell him he could stuff his wants, he gave a little bow. "What would you like?"

Oh, damn him for trying. It should make her happy, but it only made her mad. She whirled away from him. Because she didn't *know* what she wanted beyond *him*, and the past few days had made it painfully clear that there was no simple way to be together. Between his brother, her father, and royal kingdoms, things were complicated.

Add a few kidnappings into the mix and it went *beyond* complicated.

But before she could think of what to say, how to put it into words, Danil moved into the room, closing the door behind him, and continued on.

"I realize why you might want to return to the island, but it simply isn't safe. And in this case, safety must come before wants. *Both* of our wants."

He was not wrong. Now that she'd cooled off some, she understood that. He'd mismanaged dealing with her, but he was not acting *wrongly*. Just treating her as though she didn't matter.

So it wasn't the course of action she was angry with, it was the way he was dealing with it. And how this was the story of her life. Not *disagreeing* with everyone she loved. Simply wanting to be part of the decision-making of her own life.

She had thought he understood, but he didn't. She tried to find the words to explain that to him, but she didn't have them without coming apart at the seams. And wasn't that always the problem? When faced with a difficult feeling, a difficult situation…she hid. Closed herself away in a room or a cluster of rocks and yelled her frustrations to the ether.

She had learned long ago not to voice them to anyone, for they never mattered. A shout, a sob, any of those negative emotions had always gotten her sent away from her father.

"So you will take me to Mathav," she said, working very hard not to sound bitter. She was an adult. She was a *princess*. She should be able to handle all of this herself. She would *not* let him see everything that swirled inside of her. "And what happens then?" she said, coolly. Or tried to be cool anyway. "You return me to my father, and then what?"

His eyebrows were drawn together, his mouth a grim line. "I am asking what you want, not telling you what I will do."

What she *wanted* she could not have. That was always the story. Tears stung her eyes and she did not want to cry. Did not want to fall apart in front of him. Anyone. "I am trying to be reasonable and understand your plan. We go to Mathav. I am returned. Some of your soldiers join my father's army. Then what will you do?"

"What is it you want me to say, Elsebet? I am asking what you want and now you won't tell me?"

She stood there, silent and frustrated, because she wanted him to say he'd fight for *her*. Pledge himself to *her*. Be *hers*. Like he'd said the other night. But if she told him...

Father, I do not wish to be sent away. I want to be with you. To help you with the Kingdom.

No. She would not be pushed back there. She would not cry and feel like that little girl again. She'd cried then and what had it gotten her? Being sent off to the island to be alone. It had turned out better than being locked away in the castle, really, but it didn't make it any less lonely.

It didn't make her feel any less abandoned. "You only care for what *you* want," she shot at him instead.

He took her by the shoulders, all fierce, avenging soldier. But there was something else in his eyes. Something that tried to pierce the guard she was attempting to have over all the hard feelings in her heart.

"I am trying to *save* you," he growled. "Why can you not see this?"

Save you. Protect you.

Never was it *love you*.

"You want me to ask you what you want. You want me to come to you and *ask*, but you do not want a discussion. *You* do not want to ask *me*. You want to hide away in your rocks and have everyone else think that you are fine and well and above it all."

The lump in her throat kept growing.

"What is it you want if you do not want me to save you from those who would harm you?" Danil demanded.

"It will harm me to return to Mathav and not have

you." She knew she should not have said this, and still, against all better knowing, she hoped. Hoped he would understand. Hoped he would say the words.

Instead, his face went blank. And cold. He dropped her shoulders and stepped back.

"I have already been one man's toy. I will not now be yours."

Those words were like a slap against the strange panic rising within her. A *toy*? "What does that mean?"

"Just because you are a *princess*, Elsebet, does not mean you can *have* me."

She found herself speechless. And hurt. Why did he think that? How had this turned out to be just what she wanted, and twisted wrong in so many ways?

He looked at her coolly now. Like a man uninterested. "Tell me plain. What is it you want, Elsebet?"

You. You. You. "I want to go home," she managed, her throat too tight. A desperate handle on the tears threatening.

He nodded sharply. "Then I will take you home."

Danil jerked the door open, a kind of painful hurt and anger twisting inside of him, but he could not force himself to walk out. Because something was not right. Something didn't add up. Like a mission missing a piece, or an army not properly motivated. The sense that he was *missing* something.

He looked back, expecting to see her icy or angry, standing there like a princess who was sending the commoner away.

Instead, her chin was at her chest, and one tear tracked down her cheek. His heart ached. He could not leave her. Even if he did not understand what this was, he could not walk away.

So he retraced his steps, took her face in his hands and tilted it up to face him. Her eyes stubbornly refused to meet his.

"Please go," she rasped. Like she was the one with trauma to her vocal cords.

He remembered, in clear detail, that night on the beach. Where she'd yelled and cried and kicked rocks. Thinking she was alone. Isolated. Not wanting anyone to see what she truly felt. And he thought he understood now, what all this was about.

She was afraid. That he did not feel the same? That her hard feelings would send him away? He was not certain of *what* caused her fear, but he knew it was there. Was sure of it.

He used his thumb to brush away the tear on her cheek. "Why do you hate for anyone to see you hurt?"

She kept her eyes resolutely downcast though he had tilted her chin up in his hands. "It is no one's fault if I hurt."

But he had hurt her. He might not understand it, but in trying to save her, he had hurt her feelings. "Is it not? You treat me as if I have wronged you, but I do not understand how. You will have to tell me, Elsebet. I am in the dark."

She swallowed, but resolutely did not speak. The tears kept falling though, and he wiped each one away, his heart feeling bruised that she would have such anguish inside of her and be so unable to explain it.

"What are you so afraid of?" he asked, trying to work through things from her perspective. "That I would send you away?"

Her chin came up, and though the tears were there, that fierceness was in her as well. "You did! You are! You sent me away from Gintaras while you stayed behind. You are taking me back to my father." She pushed him away and he let her. "What was I meant to think?" she demanded, turning her back on him. "I know my emotions are too much. I know that I should not cry or yell. I know that begging never works."

He watched the stiff line of her back. "When I found you crying on the beach screaming and going on, what did I do?"

Her eyebrows drew together, as though she did not understand the question. But she answered it. "You kidnapped me for your brother."

It wasn't funny, but he found the odd urge to laugh. "No, I watched. I rather enjoyed the impressive show. And then I tried to convince you to come with me. When Peet made the signal, I remembered myself. My duty. But in the moment, nothing about your outburst changed what I wanted, how I felt."

She chewed on her bottom lip, clearly confused by this.

"Is this about when your father sent you to the island?"

She looked away, but she answered him. Quietly. An attempt at stoicism that turned into more tears.

"I only wanted to stay. I only wanted for him to let me help. I did not want to be sent away. Why must everyone always send me away?"

He could not hold himself apart, though maybe that would have been better. But he needed to touch her, hold her, press his words into her so she believed them. "I do not *wish* to send you away, Elsebet. I have changed the entire course of my life for having met you. For loving you. Nothing else but this giant force would have changed what I had been conditioned to believe."

She blinked once, her siren eyes wide and surprised. "You...love me?"

"I have loved very little in this life, but that small taste... It gives me no doubts now. I love you, Elsebet. I would do anything for you. Except allow you to be harmed by anyone. That is the only reason I sent you away. I needed to know my brother could not touch you. And perhaps..." He sighed. "Elsebet, you are a princess, and I am but a soldier. I may have some money, and a fleet of ships, an army at my disposal, but this does not make me royal. It does not give me what your father might want for his princess. It isn't *befitting* a princess."

She fully turned to face him now. Eyes bright, full of emotion. No, not just any emotion. *Love*. Because she was good at this. If it was a positive feeling, she showed it with no concern or attempt to hide. She could be the kindest, the sweetest, the most loving.

It was all those darker emotions that seemed to be a struggle. And as he had dealt with his stepfather's reaction to anger, he understood. The man had turned him into a tool. Had used his love for his mother against him. *Don't you want your mother to have a better life?*

So he'd gone along. Faced the King. Almost died. And learned that loving someone was a weapon. Being a tool was all that mattered.

Elsebet had begged her father to stay, to have what she wanted, and been sent away. She had learned that being upset got you punished, having wants were off-putting.

Once again, on the inside, they were the same. But they were quite different on the outside.

"Danil, I do not care who you have been. I do not care what my father wants for Mathav. I care that our love is big, important."

"*Our* love?" he asked, those last vestiges of an old ice around his heart fully melting.

Her mouth curved and she took his hands in her small ones. "I love you. Even if you did try to kidnap me. Twice."

"I did not *try*. I succeeded."

This made her laugh, which he knew was a little dark, but they were here and she… She loved him, the bastard son of a king who should have been killed.

"I am an unwanted bastard with blood on his hands." He held them up, as though she could see the blood there.

But she shook her head, pressed a kiss to each palm. "You are wanted here. You helped Win in the kitchen when you were injured. You looked at my art as though it mattered. And though you kidnapped me, though you served your brother, when faced with the right choices, you made them. You let yourself love." Her eyes tracked over his face, then she smiled that siren smile, full of secrets and power. "My father will understand. If he doesn't, we will fight until he does."

"I will fight for you, my love. If that is what you want. But you must not be afraid. To hurt in front of me. To trust me with all that you are. I want your tears and your anger and your hurt as much as your love and joy and kindness. I want all of you. Always."

Her eyes studied him, big and dark blue. Siren that she was, but his. He could see it in her eyes. They had given each other something they had been missing. Opened up new sides of each other.

She had brought him back to life, and now he was strong enough to be everything she needed.

"I love you, Danil. No matter what. I am yours and you are mine. This will be what we fight for."

"Forever, my siren."

EPILOGUE

AND IT WAS FOREVER. King Alfred of Mathav was skeptical, of course, but he had never seen his daughter quite so determined or sure as she was when they arrived on Mathav the next day.

They had been met by a hostile force that was both smaller and weaker than Danil's own. When they landed ashore, Elsebet demanded her father be summoned at once. Then she marched along, pulling Danil with her, up to the castle gates.

There were many people trailing them, asking pleading questions of Elsebet, demanding to know who Danil was.

Neither of them spoke or answered anything. They simply marched on until Elsebet burst into her father's office. He was already on his feet, angrily speaking to someone, until Elsebet entered.

His entire face changed. From a dark, ferocious anger to utter shock. Then he moved forward and pulled Elsebet into his arms. "My sweet. You're here. You're whole." He pulled her back, studied her face. "Are you unharmed?"

"Yes, Father. Thanks to Danil." She looked back at him.

But the King's expression hardened once more. "This is the man who kidnapped you." King Alfred tried to maneuver Elsebet behind him, as if he could form some kind of wall of protection. But Princess Elsebet Thore would not be maneuvered.

Ever again.

"This is the man who saved me, Father. And I wish to marry him. Soon."

King Alfred's mouth swung open in shock, and stayed there, as Elsebet relayed the events of the past few days.

Leaving out certain…parts.

Before she finished, King Alfred had needed to take a seat. Now he sat, looking up at his daughter, and the man who'd kidnapped her. And set her free.

He sighed heavily as Elsebet concluded her story with the same sentence. "I wish to marry him. Soon."

There was only a drawn-out silence for long minutes. But Elsebet did not move. Did not endeavor to beg her father or anything else. She stood, chin high, hand in Danil's. And waited.

"I have tried for the past year to find you a husband. One who could be an ally to Mathav. An asset. But also one who would treat you with fairness and kindness. And the very few times I began to consider someone, I could only think of your mother." King Alfred looked down at his hands, where he still wore his wedding ring. All these years later.

"I wanted to save you from the pain of loss." He

looked up at Elsebet, and the pain of that loss was there on his face. "But it sounds as if I've caused you a different pain along the way, and for that I am sorry."

He got to his feet once more, crossed to Elsebet and cupped her face in his hands. "She would not have wanted a political marriage for you. And I do not wish to fail you any further." His gaze slid to Danil, cool and assessing. "I cannot immediately approve such a match, but we will discuss it."

"You will approve, Father." Elsebet smiled at him, then at Danil. "I'm sure of it."

And a few weeks later, King Alfred did, just as his daughter had predicted.

"Why did you ever make such an arrangement with my brother?" Danil asked him once, after King Alfred had given his permission, but before he and Elsebet married.

The King shook his head. "I never made such a deal. I listened to his proposal, but I refused. I knew he would never be kind enough to my jewel. All I wanted for her was a life without pain and loss. A safe life."

"Life is not safe."

"No. Even locked away on a tiny island that is supposedly incapable of being breached, you might find your daughter kidnapped." The King gave him a hard look, but Danil had come to know the King.

He had built walls to hide the hurt at losing his wife, and now that Danil loved, he understood. And so had Elsebet come to understand. The ways they had hurt each other had come from love and fear.

But when you learned to accept fear and love, you no longer needed to hide.

So Danil and Elsebet were married on the island of Mathav in the great castle of Elsebet's family, with all the royal fanfare of her station. They lived many of their days on a tiny nameless island, bringing four children into the world to be taken care of by Nielson, Win and Inga, and doted on by their grandfather when they visited Mathav for holidays or political meetings.

The oldest, a girl, they named Peeta, after Danil's best friend and strongest sailor, who soon worked his way up to be the King's personal sailor. While those soldiers loyal to Danil built a strong army that protected Mathav from Aras's sad and disorganized attempts at revenge.

As years passed, laws were changed. And many years later, when Alfred passed away peacefully in his sleep as an old and beloved king, Elsebet was crowned Queen of Mathav, rather than attempt to find a royal man for her daughter to marry.

Mathav's army and her allies had grown thanks to Elsebet and Danil's efforts, and then their children's diplomatic initiatives. They were safe and whole and their family had become a dynasty. Not of riches, or armies, or lands. But of love. The kind that was not afraid of tears or fights or loss, but instead felt them all, along with hugs and joy and love.

When their eldest daughter insisted on marrying the son of a farmer, they gave their blessing, remembering that day many years ago now when King Alfred had given them his blessing.

Because of love.

Love, after all, was the only duty worth committing oneself to.

* * * * *

Were you blown away by
The Forbidden Princess He Craves?
Then you're sure to love these other stories
by Lorraine Hall!

The Prince's Royal Wedding Demand
Hired for His Royal Revenge
Pregnant at the Palace Altar
A Son Hidden from the Sicilian

Available now!

#4153 THE MAID'S PREGNANCY BOMBSHELL
Cinderella Sisters for Billionaires
by Lynne Graham
Shy hotel maid Alana is so desperate to clear a family debt that when she discovers Greek tycoon Ares urgently needs a wife, she blurts out a scandalous suggestion: *she'll* become his convenient bride. But as chemistry blazes between them, she has an announcement that will inconveniently disrupt his well-ordered world... She's having his baby!

#4154 A BILLION-DOLLAR HEIR FOR CHRISTMAS
by Caitlin Crews
When Tiago Villela discovers Lillie Merton is expecting, a wedding is nonnegotiable. To protect the Villela billions, his child must be legitimate. But his plan for a purely pragmatic arrangement is soon threatened by a dangerously insatiable desire...

#4155 A CHRISTMAS CONSEQUENCE FOR THE GREEK
Heirs to a Greek Empire
by Lucy King
Booking billionaire Zander's birthday is a triumph for caterer Mia. And the hottest thing on the menu? A scorching one-night stand! But a month later, he can't be reached. Mia finally ambushes him at work to reveal she's pregnant! He insists she move in with him, but this Christmas she wants all or nothing!

#4156 MISTAKEN AS HIS ROYAL BRIDE
Princess Brides for Royal Brothers
by Abby Green
Maddi hadn't fully considered the implications of posing as her secret half sister. *Or* that King Aristedes would demand she continue the pretense as his intended bride. Immersing herself in the royal life she was denied growing up is as compelling as it is daunting. But so is the thrill of Aristedes's smoldering gaze...

HPCNMRA1023

#4157 VIRGIN'S STOLEN NIGHTS WITH THE BOSS
Heirs to the Romero Empire
by Carol Marinelli

Polo player Elias rarely spares a glance for his staff, until he meets stable hand and former heiress Carmen. And their attraction is irresistible! Elias knows he'll give the innocent all the pleasure she could want, but that's it. Unless their passion can unlock a connection much harder to walk away from...

#4158 CROWNED FOR THE KING'S SECRET
Behind the Palace Doors...
by Kali Anthony

One year ago, her spine-tingling night with exiled king Sandro left Victoria pregnant and alone. Lied to by the palace, she believed he wanted nothing to do with them. So Sandro turning up on her doorstep—ready to claim her, his heir and his kingdom—is astounding!

#4159 HIS INNOCENT UNWRAPPED IN ICELAND
by Jackie Ashenden

Orion North wants Isla's company...and her! So when the opportunity to claim both at the convenient altar arises, he takes it. But with tragedy in his past, even their passion may not be enough to melt the ice encasing his heart...

#4160 THE CONVENIENT COSENTINO WIFE
by Jane Porter

Clare Redmond retreated from the world, pregnant and grieving her fiancé's death, never expecting to see his ice-cold brother, Rocco, again. She's stunned when the man who always avoided her storms back into her life, demanding they wed to give her son the life a Cosentino deserves!

HPCNMRB1023

Get 3 FREE REWARDS!

We'll send you 2 FREE Books plus a FREE Mystery Gift.

FREE Value Over **$20**

Both the **Harlequin® Desire** and **Harlequin Presents®** series feature compelling novels filled with passion, sensuality and intriguing scandals.

YES! Please send me 2 FREE novels from the Harlequin Desire or Harlequin Presents series and my FREE gift (gift is worth about $10 retail). After receiving them, if I don't wish to receive any more books, I can return the shipping statement marked "cancel." If I don't cancel, I will receive 6 brand-new Harlequin Presents Larger-Print books every month and be billed just $6.30 each in the U.S. or $6.49 each in Canada, a savings of at least 10% off the cover price, or 3 Harlequin Desire books (2-in-1 story editions) every month and be billed just $7.83 each in the U.S. or $8.43 each in Canada, a savings of at least 12% off the cover price. It's quite a bargain! Shipping and handling is just 50¢ per book in the U.S. and $1.25 per book in Canada.* I understand that accepting the 2 free books and gift places me under no obligation to buy anything. I can always return a shipment and cancel at any time by calling the number below. The free books and gift are mine to keep no matter what I decide.

Choose one: ☐ **Harlequin Desire**
(225/326 BPA GRNA)

☐ **Harlequin Presents Larger-Print**
(176/376 BPA GRNA)

☐ **Or Try Both!**
(225/326 & 176/376 BPA CRQP)

Name (please print)

Address   Apt. #

City   State/Province   Zip/Postal Code

Email: Please check this box ☐ if you would like to receive newsletters and promotional emails from Harlequin Enterprises ULC and its affiliates. You can unsubscribe anytime.

Mail to the Harlequin Reader Service:
IN U.S.A.: P.O. Box 1341, Buffalo, NY 14240-8531
IN CANADA: P.O. Box 603, Fort Erie, Ontario L2A 5X3

Want to try 2 free books from another series? Call 1-800-873-8635 or visit www.ReaderService.com.

*Terms and prices subject to change without notice. Prices do not include sales taxes, which will be charged (if applicable) based on your state or country of residence. Canadian residents will be charged applicable taxes. Offer not valid in Quebec. This offer is limited to one order per household. Books received may not be as shown. Not valid for current subscribers to the Harlequin Presents or Harlequin Desire series. All orders subject to approval. Credit or debit balances in a customer's account(s) may be offset by any other outstanding balance owed by or to the customer. Please allow 4 to 6 weeks for delivery. Offer available while quantities last.

Your Privacy—Your information is being collected by Harlequin Enterprises ULC, operating as Harlequin Reader Service. For a complete summary of the information we collect, how we use this information and to whom it is disclosed, please visit our privacy notice located at corporate.harlequin.com/privacy-notice. From time to time we may also exchange your personal information with reputable third parties. If you wish to opt out of this sharing of your personal information, please visit readerservice.com/consumerschoice or call 1-800-873-8635. **Notice to California Residents**—Under California law, you have specific rights to control and access your data. For more information on these rights and how to exercise them, visit corporate.harlequin.com/california-privacy.

HDHP23

HARLEQUIN
PLUS

Try the best multimedia subscription service for romance · readers like you!

Read, Watch and Play.

Experience the easiest way to get the romance content you crave.

Start your **FREE TRIAL** at
www.harlequinplus.com/freetrial.